Trouble in Savannah

Made in Savannah Cozy Mystery Series

Book Five

Hope Callaghan

hopecallaghan.com

Visit my website for new releases and special offers: hopecallaghan.com

Thank you to these wonderful ladies who help make my books shine - Peggy H., Cindi G., Jean P., Wanda D., Rosmarie H. and Barbara W. for taking the time to preview *Trouble in Savannah,* for the extra sets of eyes and for catching all my mistakes.

A special thanks to my reader review team: Alice, Amary, Barbara, Becky, Becky B, Brinda, Cassie, Christina, Cyndi, Debbie, Denota, Devan, Francine, Grace, Jan, Jo-Ann, Joeline, Joyce, Jean K., Jean M., Kathy, Lynne, Megan, Melda, Kat, Linda, Lynne, Pat, Patsy, Paula, Renate, Rita, Rita P, Shelba, Tamara and Vicki.

TABLE OF CONTENTS

Chapter 1

"Hit the brake! The brake, not the gas!" Mercedes yelled, as they sped toward the back of a big dump truck.

Carlita's seatbelt locked as she desperately stomped her foot in the direction of what she hoped was the brake.

The car came to a screeching halt, mere inches from the bed of the truck.

Mercedes' seatbelt didn't lock and her forehead made a loud *thunk* as it took a direct hit against the dashboard. "Ouch."

"Oh my gosh, Mercedes. I'm sorry." Carlita said as the dump truck rumbled on and the car behind them began to honk impatiently. "I'm going, I'm going," she muttered under her breath as she pressed her foot on the gas pedal.

Mercedes had been attempting to teach her mother to drive. Carlita had warned her daughter she didn't think they should wander out of Walton Square, their neighborhood, but Mercedes was excited her mother had finally agreed to get behind the wheel and decided they should keep going.

She was beginning to regret the decision.

"Let's go home," mother and daughter said in unison.

"We'll try again in a couple days," Mercedes added.

Carlita didn't answer, but in her mind, her driving lessons were over. She'd come within inches of rear-ending a dump truck and it would've been all her fault.

The car behind her, impatient because she wasn't driving fast enough, began tailgating them. Carlita gripped the steering wheel as she glanced in the rearview mirror.

"Ignore them," Mercedes said. "The speed limit is only 25."

When they reached the alley behind the apartment, Carlita eased the Lincoln town car into the empty parking spot and peered through the front windshield. "I think this is good."

Mercedes glanced out the passenger side window. The car was mere inches from one of the tenant's compact cars and there wasn't enough room for her to squeeze out. "You're too close on this side."

"I am?" Carlita craned her neck as she gazed out Mercedes' window. "Are you sure? It looks good to me."

"Positive. Try again."

Carlita mumbled under her breath as she shifted the car into reverse and backed up. She steered to the left and slowly pulled into the spot. This time she was too close to her son, Tony's car. Thankfully, the third try was the charm. She shut the engine off and opened the door. Her legs wobbled as she slid onto the gravel drive. "I think I'll stick to walking."

"No way." Mercedes shook her head. "You have to keep practicing."

"Downtown Savannah is made for walking," Carlita said. Mother and daughter had moved to Savannah after discovering Carlita's deceased husband, Vinnie, Sr., had left the property to his wife of almost forty years.

It wasn't the only reason they had moved from Queens, New York to Savannah. Carlita had promised her husband on his deathbed to get their two oldest sons out of the family business...the mafia family business to be exact.

It had been several months since Vinnie's sudden death and Carlita had managed to convince her middle son, Tony, to join them. Her oldest son, Vinnie Jr., still wasn't on board.

Carlita had hoped after her eldest son's recent run-in with a New York mafia boss he would change his mind and decide to pack up and move to Savannah but it had been the complete opposite.

Her son gave the "don" time to cool off and then promptly drove back to New York. Carlita had tried every trick in the book, including inviting Autumn Winter, a family friend and young woman Vinnie had showed some interest in, to dinner to try to entice him to make the move but all of Carlita's efforts had failed.

At least he had stayed long enough to help her during the grand opening of *Swag in Savannah,* Carlita's new pawnshop. So far, business hadn't been "booming" but it was steady and she couldn't complain. Between the income from the pawnshop and her apartment rental units, they were making a tidy profit.

Carlita locked the car doors, and mother and daughter wandered down the alley to the back entrance. "We got a couple more on-line applications from the ad you placed in the Savannah Evening News."

She still had a vacant apartment to rent. It was the one behind Carlita and Mercedes' unit. When Carlita finally accepted the fact Vinnie wasn't going to move, she asked her daughter to place an ad.

There had been a lot of interest in the two bedroom, one bath unit but so far, none of them had panned out. The prospective tenants either wanted to talk her down on the monthly rental rate or wanted to make payments on the security deposit and first month and last months' rent. The last one she'd talked to was a definite 'no' when he asked if pets were allowed...a pet tarantula to be exact.

Carlita promptly told the applicant she did not allow "exotic" pets and then added an addendum to the rental agreement. The landlord business was a tougher gig than she'd ever imagined. She thought about her tenant, Elvira Cobb, a perfect example of a trying tenant.

While Elvira tried every level of Carlita's patience, her other tenant, Shelby Townsend, was the complete opposite.

"Do you want me to go over the new applications?" Mercedes asked as she held the back door for her mother.

"No." Carlita shook her head. "I'll do it." Although she appreciated everything her daughter did, Carlita was determined to handle as much of the rental business on her own as possible. She secretly hoped Mercedes would one day meet someone and marry, and Carlita wanted to be able to stand on her own two feet without depending on her children.

She cast a glance at the entrance leading to the rear of the pawnshop. "I'm going to check on Tony." She'd left her son to run the pawnshop while Mercedes took her mother on her first, and perhaps last, driving lesson.

She slipped into the back of the pawnshop and spotted Tony standing behind one of the jewelry counters. He was showing a couple a display tray of men's gold rings.

She waited off to the side while the man tried on every single ring in the tray and then told Tony he'd have to think about it, right after he tried to get Tony to take less money for one of them. Carlita beamed with pride as Tony thanked the man for the interest but told him he could not go down more than twenty bucks.

The couple exited the store and Carlita wandered over to the display case. "How is business?"

Tony shrugged. "It's a little slow. Now that summer is over, I think the tourists coming into Savannah have dropped off, at least during the week. We'll have to see if it picks up on the weekends."

Carlita's gaze drifted to one of the pawnshop's new employees, Adele Ketman. She lowered her voice. "How is Adele working out?" Tony had recently hired three part-time employees with the plan they would eventually move one of them into a full-time position once the business was able to support another full-timer.

"I've finished training her and she's doing a good job," Tony said. A customer entered the store and Adele wove her way around a rack of video games to greet the shopper. She made her way over a short time later to borrow Tony's key to the display cases.

Tony handed her the keys and waited for her to walk away. "Josh seems to be catching on quick. He has a good eye for picking out merchandise and you don't have to ask him to do something. He just jumps in and does it."

"What about the other girl?" Carlita asked.

"Melody?" Tony asked. "She's only worked one shift and is still in training."

"I'm glad it's working out," Carlita smiled and patted her son's arm. "Would you like to come upstairs and have dinner with Mercedes and me tonight? I'm making linguine," she enticed.

Carlita's grandmother had handed down the recipe to her mother and then to her.

It was a Garlucci family favorite, made-from-scratch linguine with garlic, chopped fresh tomatoes and basil, not to mention a couple other "secret ingredients."

Tony grinned and patted his stomach. "Ah, Ma. I've gained at least ten pounds since I moved here."

"You could stand to put on a few pounds," Carlita said. "Would you like me to invite Shelby and Violet?" Tony and Shelby, one of Carlita's tenants, had started dating, but it was a slow go, mostly on Shelby's end. She had a sneaking suspicion it had something to do with Shelby's ex-husband.

"She's not home." Tony's smile faded. "She said she had something important to take care of after work and wouldn't be home until later this evening. I think something is going on."

Carlita frowned. "Oh dear. I hope everything is all right."

"Me too."

Loud voices interrupted their conversation and Carlita turned toward the commotion. A red-faced Adele hurried toward them. She was carrying a pocket watch. "The customer who just came in said this watch was stolen from his house last week, after someone broke in and robbed him."

Chapter 2

Carlita's heart plummeted and she stared at her son.

"I swear I know nothing about this." Tony reached for the pocket watch. "How does he know it's his?"

"There's an inscription on the back." Adele flipped the watch over and tapped the back.

Carlita squinted her eyes. "WON."

The man strode over to join them. "William Orville Nesbitt." He whipped his wallet out of his back pocket and pulled out his driver's license. "I've been visiting every pawnshop in the county, searching for this pocket watch, among other things." He turned to the woman who followed behind him.

"Check the rest of the display cases and shelves of merchandise. There's probably more of our stuff in here."

The woman nodded and began combing the aisles.

A knot formed in the pit of Carlita's stomach when the woman abruptly stopped. "I see your box of baseball cards right here." She plucked a box from the shelf and held it up triumphantly.

Tony set the watch on the counter. "Prove it."

The woman hurried over and handed it to Nesbitt, who studied the exterior of the box. "This is mine. I'll bet a hundred bucks my signed Mark McGwire card is in here." He lifted the lid and began shuffling through the cards. "Aha!" He plucked a card from the box and held it up.

Tony and Carlita stood off to the side and watched in disbelief as the couple searched the rest of the store. They moved back and forth, as they began piling merchandise on top of one of the display cases.

By the time they finished, they added a baseball bat, a DeWalt cordless drill, an Xbox, some video games and a diamond necklace the woman found in one of the display cases.

Carlita refused to let the man take the items with him and instead, insisted they call the police to file a report. She was new at the business and wasn't sure what they would do, but it beat letting a stranger walk into the store and walk out with merchandise they had paid good money for.

For all she knew, the man had been in the store earlier, casing the joint and then came back to accuse them of selling stolen goods. She still couldn't explain the initials on the pocket watch but she pushed the thought aside and reached for her cell phone.

"You call the police and I'm contacting the local news to tell them this is a crooked pawnshop," the man threatened.

Carlita slowly set the phone down and turned to her son. "Give him the stuff."

Tony shot the man a death look and shoved the "stolen" items across the counter. "Take it and leave. Don't ever come in here again."

The man and woman snatched the merchandise off the counter. "I have half a mind to contact the local news anyway."

Tony took a menacing step forward and the man picked up the pace as he hurried to the exit, passing by Elvira, who was making her way inside.

"Business must be booming and you ran out of store bags," she said after the couple made a hasty retreat.

Elvira had been opposed to Carlita opening a pawnshop and had even gone as far as requesting the Savannah Architectural Society to help stop the business from obtaining its license, claiming that as not only a tenant, but also a citizen of Savannah, a pawnshop would attract "riff raff."

"Not quite," Carlita muttered and then quickly changed the subject. "Why are you coming in through the pawnshop and not the apartment entrance in back?"

"I was heading out to run some errands but there's a delivery truck parked directly behind me and they're blocking my car. You need to ask them to move." She shifted her purse. "We're gonna need more parking spots if you plan to rent out the last apartment."

Carlita ignored the comment. "I'll ask them to move." She headed for the back door. Elvira was hot on her heels.

"I have a friend, Cool Bones, he's lookin' for a place to hang his hat and I told him about this place."

Carlita reached for the door handle. "Cool Bones?"

"His real name is Charles Benson but his stage name is Cool Bones."

"Huh. What does Cool Bones do for a living?"

"He sings jazz down at the Thirsty Crow. That's how I met him. He's a cool dude. Here's his card." Elvira fumbled around inside her purse, pulled out a card and handed it to Carlita.

"I'll think about it." Carlita shoved the card in her pocket. She had no intention whatsoever of letting one of Elvira's friends move into the empty unit. If the "friend" was anything like Elvira, the last thing she needed was her tenant's twin. "I have some other applications I'm sifting through."

"Suit yourself." Elvira shrugged. "Once word gets out this place attracts dead bodies, it's going to be tough to find a tenant. In fact, I might have to re-negotiate my monthly rent."

The tips of Carlita's ears burned. This wasn't the first time Elvira had hinted she wanted her monthly rental rate reduced but it wasn't going to work. In fact, she should be charging her tenant more...a pain in the rear fee. "We've already discussed this," she said calmly. "You're more than welcome to move out and I'll terminate the lease."

"I-I'm not saying I want to move," Elvira stuttered. "Never mind. Don't bother asking the delivery driver to move. I'll ask him myself." She hurried down the small hall and out the back door.

"She's a trip," Tony said as Elvira slammed the door behind her.

Carlita didn't have time to answer as another couple wandered into the store to shop. "I better head upstairs and start dinner." She waited for a couple more minutes, to make sure Elvira was long gone, before heading up the steps to the apartment she shared with Mercedes.

Mercedes was nowhere in sight and when she stopped to drop her purse off in her bedroom she noticed her daughter's bedroom door was closed.

Rambo, Carlita's dog, followed her from the bedroom to the kitchen and began whining as she reached for her apron. "What? You need to go out."

Rambo whined again.

"We better go before I start working on dinner." The pooch led the way to the alley out back. Rambo knew where he was going...the only green spot left on the property. It was the spot Elvira insisted Carlita turn into another parking spot but she just couldn't. Rambo had such a small sliver of green grass it would break her heart to take it away from him.

Although Morrell Park was only a short walk from the apartment, having the green space was much more convenient when Carlita didn't have time to walk that far, like now.

Rambo sniffed the tires of Tony's car and then trotted between his car and Carlita's as he headed to the grassy patch. After he took care of business, they circled the block. She rounded the last corner and nearly ran into a man headed in the opposite direction.

Carlita jumped back while Rambo lunged forward and let out a low growl, his teeth bared. "Rambo!" Rambo rarely growled at anyone. She reached for his collar, wishing she'd remembered to bring his leash.

She herded him off to the side to let the man pass as they shuffled toward the back door.

The man abruptly stopped. "I'm looking for the owner of this property."

Carlita shooed Rambo into the hall before closing the door behind him. "I'm the owner, Carlita Garlucci."

A slight smile crossed his face. "I responded to an ad via email for an apartment for rent this morning but decided to stop by and check it out myself." The man lifted his gaze and stared at the back of the building. "You're in an ideal location, convenient to downtown." He lowered his gaze and his eyes met Carlita's. "Have you rented the unit?"

"I…" A warning bell sounded somewhere in the back of Carlita's head, telling her to say 'yes,' but before she could stop herself she said, "No. Not yet."

"Would you mind if I take a look at the unit while I'm here?"

"I-I guess not." Carlita opened the door. "Follow me."

Rambo was long gone and the back door to the pawnshop was open. She started up the steps and the man trailed behind. "I apologize for springing this on you. I'm camping out on my friend's sofa so I'm kind of in a bind to find an apartment."

"It's okay." They stopped at the top of the stairs. "I'll be right back." She reached for the door handle. "I'm sorry. I didn't catch your name." Carlita was quite certain the man hadn't given her his name.

"Ben Cutler. I just started working at the Internal Revenue Service office downtown. I moved here from Roanoke. Would you like to see my picture id?" he teased.

Carlita smiled. "No. Ben. Not yet, anyway. I'll be right back." She slipped inside the apartment, returning moments later with the key in hand. "The rent is $1500 per month," she said as they made their way to the vacant unit.

Carlita hadn't been inside the unit for several days, not since she'd dragged Vinnie inside in an effort to persuade him to stay.

She gave Ben a quick tour and he said very little as she explained he would be responsible for all of his own utilities, that pets were allowed but stressed by pets, she meant cats and dogs...not an exotic or uninsurable breed.

When they finished the tour, Ben stood in the hall while Carlita locked the door. "I received several other applications and haven't had a chance to go over them yet. Would you like me to consider you as a tenant?"

Ben nodded and reached inside his pocket, pulling out a thick wad of hundred dollar bills. "As I said, I'm staying with a friend and am anxious to move as soon as possible." He licked the tip of his index finger and flipped through the bills. "I can give you first month's rent, last month's rent and the security deposit."

Ben counted the bills and held them out. "There's an extra five hundred bucks for your trouble."

Carlita stared at the money. It was five thousand dollars in cold, hard cash. For the second time in a row, she almost said 'no,' but before she could stop herself, she nodded. "Of course, I'll need to review your application." Carlita took the money and folded it in half. "I'll hang onto this until I make a decision."

"Let me get a receipt." She didn't wait for an answer as she hurried inside her apartment and grabbed the receipt booklet from her desk along with an ink pen. She scribbled out his name and the dollar amount after carefully counting the bills. She returned to the hall where Ben Cutler stood waiting. "I'll give you an answer tomorrow," she promised.

Carlita walked him to the end of the hall. "I trust I have your application in my email but if you don't hear from me by...say three o'clock tomorrow afternoon, please call." She jotted her cell phone number on the bottom of the receipt and handed it to him.

Mr. Cutler assured her he would as he followed her down the steps and into the alley. Carlita waited until he was around the corner and out of sight before stepping back inside and slowly closing the door.

There was something about the man, something that didn't quite sit right and the first thing she planned to do was go over his application with a fine-tooth comb.

Chapter 3

"I need some help."

Annie Dowton, the owner of *Riverfront Real Estate,* a real estate office catty-corner to Carlita's place, leaned forward in her chair. "What kind of help? Don't tell me you've found another body."

Cindy, Annie's assistant, chuckled. "It's been pretty quiet around here for at least a couple weeks now. Surely Carlita has something up her sleeve to liven things up."

Carlita slumped into an empty chair and rolled her eyes. *If they only knew.* "I need to rent out the apartment behind mine ASAP." She explained Vinnie had returned to New York after insisting he did not intend to move to Savannah, at least not yet and Elvira had suggested her friend, Cool Bones, was looking for a place to live.

Cindy interrupted. "Cool Bones. I've heard the name before." She hopped out of her chair. "Is he a singer?"

"Yeah. Elvira told me he's a jazz singer. Do you know him?"

"I know of him. He plays at one of the local nightclubs. A couple years back he was involved in some sort of scandal and the police got involved. I can't remember exactly what it was now..."

"Maybe you should 'x' him off the list," Annie said.

Carlita chuckled. "That doesn't bother me. I bet I've been investigated more by the police than he has."

She continued. "The fact that Elvira suggested him, now that makes me want to 'x' him off the list. I also had a man show up on my doorstep, interested in renting the apartment," Carlita said. "He gave me the first month's rent, last month's rent and the security deposit...in cash. I told him I would hold onto the money but would have to go over his application first."

Annie held up a hand. "Carlita. You should know better."

"I know but I had the cash in hand. It was hard to turn down." She'd done something similar when Elvira had strong-armed her into letting her move in. "I must have "sucker" tattooed on my forehead, which is why I'm here. Something about the guy makes me uneasy. He said he just took a job working for the IRS downtown."

"The IRS?" Annie's eyes widened. "You want an IRS employee living under your roof?"

"Not really." Carlita leaned forward and placed the palms of her hands on the top of Annie's desk. "I need help. I need a tenant, a good tenant, and fast."

"I'll start searching through recent rental inquiries right now." Cindy slid into her chair and reached for her mouse.

"Thanks Cindy."

Annie changed the subject. "How is *Swag in Savannah* doing? Every time I go by, the place looks busy."

"It's been great, up until this morning when a customer came in claiming we were selling items that were stolen from his home. Tony assured me he thoroughly checks out any merchandise coming into the shop." Carlita shook her head. "It looks like some fenced goods might have slipped through."

It was one more thing to worry about and the thought depressed Carlita. The pawnshop was barely on its feet and now this. The women discussed the business and Annie tossed out a few ideas for Carlita to set safety measures in place to avoid another incident of questionable purchases.

Carlita glanced at her watch. "I better get going." She stood.

"I found a couple promising applicants already and just forwarded them to Annie," Cindy said. "She can contact them to see if they're still interested in downtown apartments."

Annie followed Carlita to the door. "I'll call them this afternoon and will email the ones I think look promising."

"Thanks Annie." Carlita exited the office and stepped onto the sidewalk. As she crossed the street, she noticed a familiar figure leaving the pawnshop and strolling down the sidewalk. It was Ben Cutler.

She hurried into the shop and made a beeline for the back, where Tony was ringing up a customer purchase. Carlita waited until the customer paid for their purchases and left. "There was a man in here a few minutes ago. He was tall with dark hair and on the thin side. What was he doing?"

Tony shrugged. "He was lookin' around. Didn't buy anything. He asked a couple questions about selling some stuff. Said he was trying to clean out a storage unit and was getting ready to move."

"What kind of stuff?" Carlita asked.

"The usual...gold, electronics. Why?"

Carlita lowered her voice. "Because he just handed me a pile of cash and told me he was looking for a place to live. He also said he just took a job with the IRS downtown."

Tony frowned. "The IRS? They're just as bad as the cops. You ain't gonna rent to him, are you?"

"Not if I can help it. I just left Annie's place. She's going to try to help me find a tenant ASAP."

Carlita changed the subject. "Have you heard anything else from that man, Nesbitt, and his stolen goods?"

"Nope." Tony shook his head. "He mighta been a scammer. I say we have a 50/50 of never hearing from him again."

Carlita hadn't thought of that angle. "Scamming? How?"

"You know. Claims the merchandise was his and instead of running the risk of him contacting the local news, we give him the goods. End of story."

"Like bribing us so he'll go away?" Carlita clutched her chest. "I've never heard of such a thing."

"Welcome to the world of business," Tony said.

A customer approached, carrying a pair of cowboy boots.

"I'll see you later." Carlita made her way up the stairs and into the empty apartment. She hung her keys on the hook and headed to the patio to grab a few tomatoes off the vine.

She'd been thrilled when she discovered she could grow tomatoes in South Georgia late in the year, even into early December if it was warm enough.

There was plenty of sunshine on one section of her deck for the vegetables to thrive and as she reached down to pluck the ripe tomatoes; a flicker of sunshine warmed her face. She hadn't spent a winter in the south but was looking forward to mild winter days and cool winter nights versus the frigid freezing temperatures of New York.

Carlita wouldn't miss the snow and the ice and she smiled as she realized she was actually looking forward to wintertime. The smile quickly faded when she thought about the fact this would be her first Christmas without Vinnie.

Rambo nudged Carlita's arm and she patted his head. "You like the nice weather too, huh?"

She left the patio door open and made her way into the kitchen to start on her linguine. One of

Carlita's favorite things about her linguine was how easy it was to make.

Carlita had spent an entire morning the previous week whipping up batches of linguine and spaghetti noodles. She pulled a bag of the pasta from the freezer to thaw while she sautéed the garlic in olive oil before adding chopped olives, tomatoes and other ingredients.

She reached into the pantry for a loaf of crusty Italian bread. The shelf was empty. Carlita could've sworn she'd picked up two loaves of bread the other day when she stopped by Colby's Corner Store.

Rambo trotted into the kitchen and stuck his nose in the pantry.

Carlita glanced at her pooch. "Did you eat my loaves of bread?"

She grabbed the box of dog treats, shook a handful into the palm of her hand and held them out. "I'm going to have to start locking up the food so it doesn't wander off."

Carlita eyed the pasta sitting on the counter. "I can't have homemade pasta without crusty bread." She shut the stove off, removed her apron and hung it on the hook before covering the dish.

Luckily, she'd started dinner early and had plenty of time to make a quick trip to Colby's for more bread. She closed the patio door before grabbing her keys and making her way out of the apartment.

When she reached the bottom of the stairs, she contemplated telling Tony she was running to the store but changed her mind when she stuck her head inside and spotted him behind the gun counter waiting on a customer.

"I hope he remembers the paperwork this time," she muttered under her breath as she pulled the door shut. Tony hadn't grasped the concept that anyone who attempted to purchase a gun at their store had to pass a background check before they were allowed to leave with their purchase. She caught him almost letting a customer leave last week without processing the paperwork.

It made her wonder if the guns Tony owned were legal purchases. Maybe she didn't want to know.

A stiff breeze whipped around the side of the building and Carlita picked up the pace as she passed by *Shades of Ink*, Steve Winters' tattoo shop.

Steve and his sister, Autumn, were the first two people Mercedes and she had met when they arrived in Savannah to check out their new properties.

On more than one occasion, Carlita caught a flicker of interest in Steve's eyes when he was around Mercedes and she suspected he had a crush on her daughter, which Mercedes vehemently denied.

Steve was inside his shop, hunched over a man lying on the table. He didn't look up as she passed by. When she reached the corner, she turned right and nearly collided with a young couple studying a street map...tourists.

She shifted to the right and then hurried inside Ken Colby's grocery store. The smell of freshly baked bread filled the air and she sniffed appreciatively.

Faith, Ken's daughter, was standing behind the front cash register and she waved when she spotted Carlita.

Carlita smiled as she plucked a handbasket from the rack and made a beeline for the back where the baked goods display was located. On her way, she grabbed a bottle of ranch dressing and a bag of potato chips.

"Your favorite Italian bread is hot out of the oven," a voice echoed from behind the meat counter.

"You must have read my mind." Carlita placed two loaves inside her basket before wandering to the meat counter. "If I didn't know better, I could swear my bread grows legs and sneaks off in the middle of the night."

Ken grinned. "Maybe you have SRED."

"Huh?"

"SRED. Sleep-related eating disorder. It's a disorder where you reach a state of being semi awake and start eating. When you wake up the next morning, you don't remember a thing."

Carlita shifted the basket and patted her hips. "So that's why I'm packing on the pounds. I have SRED."

She ordered some shaved roast beef and turkey before heading toward the checkout. Carlita dropped a few more had-to-have items in her basket on the way and then placed the overflowing basket on the counter.

Faith reached for the bread. "Weren't you just in here the other day buying these same loaves of bread? You must like it."

"I love your bread," Carlita said. "And so does someone else in my house. It keeps vanishing during the night."

Faith smiled, the dimple in her chin deepening. "I bet you're a fabulous cook."

Carlita had been tossing around the idea of hosting a small soiree for some time now and planned to invite their Walton Square neighbors and business owners. "I've been meaning to host a cena and invite you and your father and the other Walton Square neighbors."

"A cena?"

"Cena is Italian for dinner."

Faith patted her stomach. "Sounds delish." She scanned the packets of meat and placed them inside an empty grocery bag.

Carlita quickly warmed to the idea. "I'm thinking maybe next Saturday or Sunday evening. I'll need to make sure Mercedes is available to help."

Faith finished scanning Carlita's purchases and placed them in a second bag. "It sounds wonderful. Dad and I don't get out much anymore. We..." Faith's voice trailed off.

Carlita had always wondered about the Colbys. She'd never seen nor heard father or daughter ever mention Faith's mother and although she was curious, she didn't want to pry. If...and when they wanted to talk about it, they would. After all, everyone had skeletons in their closet. Heaven only knew how many Carlita and her family had. In fact, they had so many skeletons she was surprised the door would even shut.

"Sunday might work best since we close the store early on Sundays, but again, I'll need to check with Mercedes first."

A smile beamed across Faith's face as she handed Carlita her bags. "It sounds great Mrs. Garlucci. We'd love to come, or at least I would."

Carlita stepped out onto the sidewalk, her mind whirling at the thought of a dinner party.

She could invite Annie and of course, Cindy, Steve and Autumn Winter, the Colbys. There was also her new neighbor, John Alder, who recently purchased the former Walton Square Souvenir shop. Her pulse quickened at the thought of John. It happened every time she thought of her new neighbor and his mesmerizing smile.

John's father had built the home, the former souvenir shop, for his family many years ago. There had been a family tragedy when John and his sister were young and their father raised the two siblings alone. After graduation, John had moved away from Savannah but recently returned and purchased the home his father had built with plans to turn it into a bed and breakfast.

He had stopped by Savannah Swag not long after they opened but it had been so hectic that day they hadn't had a chance to talk and she hadn't seen him since, although she'd noticed a lot of construction going on.

John was probably as busy as Carlita. Still, it wouldn't hurt to invite him.

There was also Jan and Stu Fischer, the owners of *A Scoop in Time* ice cream shop. Last, but not least, was Pirate Pete, the owner of the *Parrot House Restaurant.* Carlita and her children had dined there recently. Pete refused to let them pay for their meal and it was time to return the favor.

Carlita picked up the pace, excited at the thought of planning her first bona fide dinner party. It would be fun.

So caught up in her musing over the party, Carlita almost collided with Steve Winter, who was standing in the doorway of his tattoo shop.

"Hello Steve."

"Hi Carlita. I thought you were going to walk right on past." He took a drag off his cigarette and blew the smoke over her head.

"I didn't know you smoked." Carlita shifted the bags she was carrying.

"I quit but started up again. It's a bad habit."

Carlita wrinkled her nose. "Yeah. Don't get me started. I've been trying to get Tony to quit for years now. I haven't seen much of you lately. How's business?" she asked.

"Business is great. Ever since you opened your pawnshop, business is booming."

"That's good," Carlita said. "Before I forget, I'm thinking about hosting a dinner party this Sunday evening and plan to invite everyone who lives and works in Walton Square."

"I'll be there with bells on." Steve grinned. "I love your food Carlita. You don't have to ask me twice." Steve had eaten with the Garlucci family several times. As a bachelor, he claimed the only time he ate a home-cooked meal was when Carlita invited him over.

She secretly suspected Steve was interested in more than Carlita's Italian cooking, and Mercedes was the real draw. "Great. I've already invited the Colbys and plan to invite Annie and Cindy, John Alder, the Fischers as well as Pirate Pete and a couple others." There was no way she could host a dinner party without inviting her tenants, Elvira and Shelby. Hopefully, Elvira would behave herself.

Carlita told Steve good-bye, but not before promising to send out Evites and hand deliver an actual invitation within the next day or two.

She quickly crossed the street, relieved that she was almost home. The bags of groceries were cutting off her circulation.

Carlita rounded the side of the building, stepped into the alley and nearly collided with a short, dark man wearing a striped three-piece suit, a stylish felt fedora perched atop his head.

The man grinned, a set of gleaming white teeth contrasting his dark, smooth skin. "Lordy you got your hands full!" He reached for the bags.

"That I do," Carlita agreed. "Can I help you?"

"Maybe," the man said. "I'm looking for Carlita Garlicky."

"I'm Carlita."

"My name is Charles Benson. My friends call me Cool Bones and one of those friends, Elvira Cobb, told me you have an apartment for rent." He grabbed her bags with one hand and lifted the hat off his head with the other. "And I just so happen to be lookin' for a place to hang my hat."

Chapter 4

Carlita's first thought was she needed to up the monthly rent for her apartments. They were apparently a very hot commodity. Her second thought was Elvira had set her up. The whole scene reminded her of how Elvira had cornered her in the exact same spot and convinced her to let her rent an apartment.

Vowing not to let Elvira catch her off guard again, Carlita shook her head. "I do have an apartment for rent and am currently taking applications but I am not making a decision until I have a chance to look at them all," she said firmly.

Charles smiled. "I completely understand. Can I help you carry your bags inside?" He motioned to the heavy bags he was now holding.

"That would be nice." Carlita relaxed slightly. The man didn't appear to be at all like Elvira. He was a lot...calmer and kinder.

Carlita unlocked the back door and Charles followed her inside. "As I said, Elvira mentioned you had an empty unit. The location is perfect since I perform down at the *Thirsty Crow* most nights." He closed the door behind them. "Do you like jazz music?"

"I don't know," Carlita admitted. "Jazz is big in New York. I'm a New Yorker - Queens to be exact - but my husband wasn't much into music."

"Ah. You're a long way from the big city down here," Charles said as they tromped up the steps. "What brought you to Savannah?"

Carlita paused when she reached the top. "That's a loaded question." She smiled. Charles' voice was smooth, soothing almost. Whereas Ben Cutler had immediately raised red flags and given Carlita an uneasy feeling, Charles had the exact opposite effect.

She gazed into his warm brown eyes. The corners crinkled, as if he smiled a lot. Charles smiled. "I don't mean to impose. I can leave the groceries here."

"Would you like to see the apartment?" Carlita asked impulsively.

"Again, I don't want to impose." Charles laughed. "Although I guess it's a little late for that."

Carlita slipped the key in the lock. "Let me drop these off inside and grab the apartment key."

She hurried into her apartment with the bags of groceries, leaving Charles in the hall. Carlita returned moments later, key in hand. "Like I said, I've had a great deal of interest in this unit but if you would like to fill out a rental application, I'll be happy to take a look at it."

"I just so happen to have it here." He reached into his front pocket, pulled out a crumpled piece of paper and handed it to Carlita. "Sorry about the wrinkled condition. I filled it out last night after my gig ended."

"No problem. I'm sure it's fine, as long as you filled it out completely."

"Yes ma'am. I did."

Carlita unlocked the rear unit door, pushed it open and stepped aside. "Would you be living here alone?"

"Yes. My daughter lives in Atlanta with my granddaughter. They come and visit every couple of months but other than that it's just me." Charles stepped to the center of the living room and slowly spun around. "This is a real nice apartment Ms. Garlicky."

"Garlucci," Carlita corrected. "For some reason, Elvira has changed my name to Garlicky."

Charles chuckled. "I'm sorry...Mrs. Garlucci."

"You can call me Carlita."

"And you can call me Cool Bones."

She showed him the rest of the apartment as they chatted about his job. Carlita quickly decided she was going to drop by the Thirsty Crow to listen to him sing. They finished the tour and stepped into the hall. She flipped the lock and pulled the door shut.

"My lease is up on my apartment at the end of the month but I would be willing to pay now and move sooner if you decide to rent to me," Cool Bones told her. "I listed my landlord as a reference. I've lived there for several years but I'm gettin' older now and these old bones don't like the long walk from the club back home."

The more Charles...Cool Bones...talked, the more Carlita liked him. She almost threw caution to the wind and told him she'd rent the apartment to him, but something held her back and that something...er...someone, was Elvira.

Carlita led him to the bottom of the stairs and they stepped out into the alley. "I plan to go over all of the applications this afternoon and will have an answer in the morning."

"I look forward to hearing from you." Cool Bones held out his hand and Carlita placed hers in his warm grasp.

"It was a pleasure meeting you Mrs. Garlucci." Cool Bones released her hand, tipped his hat, turned on his heel and strolled toward the sidewalk, whistling a catchy tune.

When she got back inside the apartment, Carlita discovered Mercedes was home and holed up in her bedroom with the door shut. She tapped lightly on her daughter's bedroom door.

The door jerked open and she jumped back as she clutched her chest. "I don't know why it still gets me every time you do that but it scares me half to death."

"Sorry Ma." Mercedes leaned her hip against the doorframe. "Where'd you wander off to?"

"I had to run over to Colby's to pick up more Italian crusty bread for dinner. I thought I had at least one loaf of bread left but it mysteriously disappeared overnight."

Mercedes lowered her gaze.

"Are you midnight snacking?" Carlita asked.

"Maybe."

"Mercedes! You ate a whole loaf of Italian bread by yourself?"

"I was burning the late night oil and had the midnight munchies," Mercedes said. "The bread is the bomb. I even experimented with this spicy Italian dip. You should try it. It has EVOO, dried oregano, basil, garlic and my secret ingredient, hot sauce."

Carlita wrinkled her nose. "Hot sauce?" She made a cross sign on her chest. "Nonna Maria would roll over in her grave if she knew you added hot sauce to Italian dip." Nonna Maria was Mercedes' grandmother on her father's side.

She changed the subject. "I'm thinking of having a cena this Sunday night and inviting all the neighbors. What do you think?"

"Oh. Our first party." Mercedes clasped her hands. "It sounds great. I'll help."

"Good. I was hoping you would say that." They briefly discussed a timeframe and then Carlita told her daughter she needed to put her groceries away.

Mercedes followed her mother to the kitchen. "Have you had any luck on the applicants for the apartment?"

"Funny you should ask." Carlita unfolded the crumpled application Charles Benson had given her and set it on the counter. "I have a few applications in my email, plus this one." She told her daughter how she had an uneasy feeling about Ben Cutler, the IRS agent and got a good feeling about Charles Benson.

"You want me to take a look at the applications?" Mercedes asked.

"Yes." Carlita nodded. "I need help. I don't want another Elvira, although Elvira was the one who told Cool Bones about the apartment."

"Cool Bones?"

"Charles Benson. He's a jazz singer down at a bar called the *Thirsty Crow*."

"We should go down there one night." Mercedes studied the front of Cool Bones' application. "This one sounds promising. I'll check it out now."

Mercedes headed to her room while Carlita finished setting the table and warming the pasta dish. By the time she finished the dinner preparations, Tony arrived and Mercedes emerged from the bedroom.

"Did you invite Shelby and Violet?" Carlita placed the silverware on the table.

"I stopped by before I came here and Shelby's still not home." Tony eased into the seat. "Maybe next time."

Carlita told her son about the dinner party tentatively scheduled for Sunday evening and he said he would have to hold down the fort at the pawnshop until six-thirty, when they closed. She turned to her daughter. "Did you have time to go through all the applications?"

Mercedes nodded. "I found four in your email. Two of them were from Annie and Cindy. One was the IRS guy and another that came in from the ad I placed. Counting Cool Bones' application, there are five altogether." She plopped down in one of the chairs. "I only did a quick check of each application but the IRS guy and Cool Bones appear to be the most promising."

Tony lifted a hand. "It's your decision, but I say if you let the IRS in the door, it's like letting the cops move in. Go with the other guy." He unfolded his napkin and tucked the edges around the neckline of his shirt.

Carlita sank into a seat opposite her son and reached for her napkin. "I have to agree with Tony. Mr. Cutler makes me uneasy. I can't quite put my finger on it. The fact he was anxious to give me all that money, in cash even, threw up a red flag. He seems desperate to rent the apartment."

"Criminals are desperate." Tony reached for the basket of sliced bread.

"I'm not saying he's a criminal," Carlita said. "After all, the government hired him."

Tony raised a brow and snorted.

Mercedes snickered.

"Okay. So he could be corrupt as they come. All I'm sayin' is if Cool Bones, Mr. Benson, is clean I think he should be our first choice."

Tony cleared his throat. "I agree." He shifted in his seat. "I was gonna wait til after dinner to tell you both but I got a little bad news. It's about the pawnshop."

Chapter 5

"W-what about the pawnshop?" Carlita asked. The last thing she needed was bad news...more bad news.

"Got a woman who came in just before I closed for the night. She wandered around the store and then all of the sudden started screaming something about her diamond watch was in our display case."

Mercedes reached for the bowl of pasta. "So? Maybe she gave it to someone and they decided it was ugly and sold it to us."

Tony shot his sister a quick glance. "I wish that was the case. She said someone broke into her house last week and the watch was one of the items that were stolen."

Carlita pounded her fist on the table. "This is the second person today. Let me guess, it wasn't the only item."

"Nope." Tony shook his head. "She also pointed out a pair of diamond earrings and matching necklace."

"What did you do?" Carlita asked.

"The first thing I did was match the product code to the list. I couldn't find the watch but I found the diamond necklace and earrings. The good news is I got a picture of the seller's identification card." Tony sighed heavily. "I haven't had time to contact him yet. I told the lady it was too late to do anything about it tonight. I took her number and promised to call her in the morning."

"What did she say?" Mercedes asked.

Tony shrugged. "She threw a fit, threatened to call the cops and I called her bluff, told her to go right ahead. Finally, she stormed out the front door but not before she said she was going to call the local news and report us to the Better Business Bureau."

The color drained from Carlita's face. Another one. It was the last thing they needed. She buried her face in her hands. "This is terrible."

Tony reached over and patted his mother's shoulder. "Don't worry Ma. I'll get to the bottom of this. Let's not panic, not yet."

The trio discussed the recent incidents at length over dinner. Carlita's appetite had vanished and she pushed her pasta around her plate before finally giving up on eating.

Tony and Mercedes attempted to cheer their mother but the knot in the pit of her stomach grew the more she thought about the 'stolen' merchandise.

"What if someone is setting us up, maybe another local pawnshop?" Mercedes wiped the corners of her mouth and set her napkin next to her empty plate. "It's too coincidental for two incidents...in the same day even."

"I smell a rat," Tony agreed.

"Maybe you're right." Carlita stared past her son and out the slider door. "What are the chances of two different people coming in on the same day with the same complaint?"

Tony pushed back his chair and stood. "I'll look into it first thing in the morning."

The trio cleared the table and loaded the dishwasher. Tony thanked his mother for dinner and then said he wanted to stop by Shelby's apartment to see if she was home before heading to his apartment to catch up on some paperwork.

Carlita thanked her son and waited until he was in the hall before closing the door. What if Tony had been careless and hadn't thoroughly checked the merchandise coming into the store?

They had opened their doors only a few short weeks ago and this was the first incident...incidents to occur. It did seem highly suspicious to have two different people with the same claim show up on the same day.

Carlita spent the rest of the evening straightening the apartment. She briefly thought about working on the invitations for the upcoming dinner party or putting together a dinner menu, but her heart wasn't in it. She was too worried about the pawnshop.

What if the woman followed through on her threat to contact the Better Business Bureau and they started to investigate Savannah Swag, or worse yet, contacted the news? Carlita didn't have anything to hide, other than a few minor or maybe major things from her family's past but those didn't directly involve her.

She thought about Tony. What if the police became involved and started digging around in Tony's background? Carlita knew very little of what her son had done in the past. She wasn't sure she wanted to know. What she did know was he was trying to get clean.

The whole situation put her on edge. By the time she finished getting ready for bed, she'd worked herself into a tizzy and lay awake half the night, worrying about her son, worrying how many more "hot" items were for sale inside their pawnshop and wondering how on earth they were going to sort through the mess.

Carlita finally fell into a fitful sleep. When she woke early the next morning, she was exhausted but wide-awake. She slipped her robe on and tiptoed into the kitchen where she started a pot of coffee.

After the coffee brewed, she carried a cup out onto the deck and eased into one of the chairs. Off in the distance, she could hear the loud blare of a car alarm. *So much for the peace and quiet of an early morning.*

She sipped her steaming coffee and set the cup on the small table next to her.

Rambo padded onto the deck and flopped down beside Carlita's chair. She reached over and patted his head. "I hope we have a better day than yesterday," she said. "I bet you're ready to go for a walk."

After she finished her coffee, she threw a pair of sweatpants and t-shirt on and brushed her teeth while Rambo patiently waited by the door.

Carlita grabbed her house keys and Rambo's leash and wandered out the back door.

The first rays of daylight were peeking over the horizon so she decided to take a walk around the block.

She waited until they were in the alley to hook Rambo's leash to his collar and then they strolled to the other end of the alley, stopping for a brief break in the grassy area next to the parking lot before making their way down the side of the building.

Her heart plummeted as she glanced at the side of the empty building, what she hoped would one day be her Italian restaurant. Carlita had decided to get the pawnshop up and running before tackling the next project, the restaurant.

Based on the way things were going, she'd be lucky if she could successfully keep the pawnshop afloat, especially if they continued to buy hot merchandise, pay good money, then turn around and hand it over to the rightful owners.

Carlita and Rambo stopped in front of the courtyard and she peered between the bars of the wrought iron gate. It had been a few days since she'd had time to enjoy the courtyard, which was a shame since Mercedes and she had spent long hours sprucing the place up.

It was a serene sanctuary smack dab in the middle of a busy city. She vowed to check on the courtyard later in the day, after it was daylight, as they moved on and continued their walk.

Carlita caught a glimpse of interior lights at John Alder's place and she could've sworn she spotted a shadowy figure move across an upper window. The construction crews had been there for several long days and Carlita wondered how the work was progressing.

She passed by the front entrance to the pawnshop. Despite the current crisis, Carlita had so many reasons to be thankful and she reminded herself of those as they walked.

"Hello." A voice echoed from the other side of the street. Someone was standing in the doorway of the Alder property, waving.

Carlita waved back and then reached up to smooth her hair, certain she looked like she'd just crawled out of bed, which she had.

John Alder crossed the street. He reached down and patted Rambo's head. "Hello Rambo."

Thank goodness it was still semi dark.

"You're up bright and early," he said.

Carlita shifted Rambo's leash to her other hand. "We couldn't sleep so we thought we would take an early walk while it was still quiet."

"I didn't mean to interrupt your peace and quiet," John apologized.

"You didn't. I mean...I didn't mean it like that." Carlita stumbled over her words. "I was going to stop by later today to invite you to a Walton Square neighborhood dinner I plan to have over at my place Sunday night."

John smiled. "It sounds great. I don't know too many of my neighbors yet. It would be a good way to meet the rest of the area business owners. What time?"

Carlita frowned. She hadn't gotten that far yet... "Around six? It's tentative and I plan to hand deliver the invitations later today or tomorrow."

"I'm free so any time works for me." He motioned toward his front door. "The crew is making great progress. Would you like a tour?"

"I..." Carlita could just envision how she appeared to John Alder. Hair not combed, wearing a tattered t-shirt and frumpy sweatpants. "As long as you leave the lights on low," she joked.

"You look beautiful," John said. "Seriously."

The tips of Carlita's ears burned and her breath caught in her throat. "I-I...wasn't fishing for a compliment but thank you," she stuttered.

Rambo led the way as the two of them crossed to the other side of the street.

John's front door was wide open and Carlita followed him inside. Workers had gutted the entire first floor, all the way down to the stud walls. As they toured, he explained his plan for the main floor.

The plans included a cozy parlor, a reception area, a formal dining room, a state-of-the-art kitchen, and a cozy breakfast nook, not to mention a hall powder room. A long hall would connect the front and back of the house.

The second floor would contain four guest suites, complete with attached baths, each boasting a cast iron claw foot tub. A large hall, similar to the one in Carlita's building, would connect the guest suites.

On the third level, he showed her what would be his private quarters, complete with an efficiency kitchen, a small dining/living combo, a bedroom and bath. Carlita followed Rambo to the window and peered out, staring right at the side of her building. "You have a great view of the side of my building."

John joined her. "Yes. I have a bird's eye view of your alley and your front sidewalk."

They retraced their steps as they made their way to the front door. "It's going to be impressive," Carlita said. "Maybe you can host some haunted tunnel tours when you open for business."

"I'll bring them to your place," John joked. He followed her onto the sidewalk. "Would you like me to walk you home?"

Carlita blushed a second time. "No. Rambo will protect me. If anyone tries to mug me, he'll lick them to death."

She promised John she would stop back by to drop off an invitation and then hurried across the street. Rambo and she stepped inside the hall and she caught a glimpse of light beaming from under Tony's apartment door.

When she knocked, there was no answer so they headed to the back of the pawnshop. It was still early and *Swag in Savannah* wasn't open yet. When she stepped inside, she found Tony sitting at the corner desk, hunched over the computer keyboard.

"You're up and at 'em early."

Tony spun around in the chair. "Ma! I didn't hear you come in."

Carlita took one look at her son's face. "What's wrong?"

Tony ran a hand through his hair. "After I got home last night, I tried to call the customer who sold me the diamond watch and other stuff."

"And?"

"Here's the info on the person who sold the necklace and earrings." Tony slid a sheet of paper to the edge of the desk. "The ID on file is Dawson Greene so I called the number. The person who answered said they'd never heard of a Dawson Greene."

Carlita shuffled forward and stared at the paper. She picked it up and squinted her eyes as she studied the photocopy of the identification card. "I wonder if this is his real address."

Tony shook his head. "Nope. I just looked it up. The address is bogus. 272 Baybridge Lane doesn't exist."

Chapter 6

Carlita sank into the chair next to her son and stared at the piece of paper. "I..."

"We've been had," Tony said as he shook his head. "I can't believe it. Me, of all people, being taken for a sucker. I thought I could sniff out a scam a mile away. I guess I'm losin' my touch."

"Where's the stuff the woman who came in last night claims belongs to her?"

Tony reached inside the drawer, pulled out a 5x7 manila envelope and handed it to his mother. "She said she was comin' in sometime this morning."

Mercedes wandered in during the conversation. "Let me take a look at the goods."

Carlita handed her daughter the seller's identification paperwork and the envelope with the jewelry. "I missed part of the conversation. Tell me again what happened."

Tony explained how a woman had come in just before he closed for the night. She claimed someone had broken into her home and stolen the watch, along with the diamond necklace and earrings.

"Did she describe the goods before she saw them?" Mercedes asked.

"To a 'T.' Like I said, it's funny cuz the watch wasn't on the list. The other items, the necklace and earrings, were tagged and priced but I don't see them in the log of purchases."

Mercedes tapped the tip of the envelope on the edge of the desk. "It could be the customer sold the items at different times. Is there any way to track sellers' names or addresses? I mean, it might be repeat sellers."

Tony snorted. "Yeah. More like repeat robbers who keep bringin' their merchandise to our place to unload. I started a database but it's not finished. I haven't been accepting pawn items yet cuz I don't have all my ducks in a row." He eyed his sister. "You're pretty good with the computer stuff. Why don't you help me finish setting up the database to track sellers and people looking to pawn?"

"All I got right now is this." He picked up a thick black binder and waved it in the air.

"I guess that's what we need to do." Mercedes took the binder from her brother, opened it up and flipped through the pages. "This is gonna take some time."

"Move over." She nudged her brother out of the chair and plopped down. "I might as well get started."

Rambo began to whine. "I'm going to head upstairs to take a shower," Carlita said. "Hopefully, the person who claims the jewelry is theirs won't show up until I get back down here. I want to hear what she has to say."

She hurried to the apartment where she quickly showered, fed Rambo and Grayvie, her cat, and then headed back to the store. The place was empty, except for Tony who stood by the front window staring out and Mercedes who was hard at work on the computer.

Carlita wandered to the window and touched her son's arm. "Why don't you take a break? You worked late last night and were up early this morning. If the woman comes in, I'll handle it." She spoke with a great deal more confidence than she felt. "Did she even bother to give you her name?"

"She was blustering so much; I couldn't get a word in edgewise. She's short, about your height. She's got curly red hair and a high-pitched voice."

Tony shifted his attention and watched as a couple strolled down the sidewalk, past the front window. "I've been meanin' to check out the flea market downtown. Maybe some fresh air will clear my head." He kissed his mother's cheek and then headed out the back door.

A trio of customers stepped inside the store and Carlita pushed aside her worries over the stolen goods. Business was brisk for most of the morning and she almost forgot about the incidents from the previous day.

Mercedes stopped working late morning, telling her mother she'd made good progress on creating a spreadsheet of sellers and then headed upstairs to check on Rambo.

Carlita was alone in the store and she wandered up and down each of the aisles, straightening items on the shelves as she walked. Josh, one of the part-time employees, arrived around noon, giving Carlita a chance to take a bathroom break and grab a quick bite to eat.

Mercedes was in the kitchen fixing sandwiches when Carlita arrived. She gazed at the row of bread slices lined up on the counter. "You must be hungry."

"I was fixing a sandwich for you and Tony, too."

"Tony still hasn't come back. Josh is holding down the fort." Carlita reached for one of the sandwiches Mercedes had just finished assembling and took a big bite. "Thanks for the food. I better get back down there."

"Did the redhead show up?"

"Not yet." Carlita shook her head. "Maybe it was a scam and she's not going to."

Carlita's cell phone beeped. It was Josh. He had sent her a text message, telling her there was a woman downstairs demanding she talk to the manager.

"I guess we're not getting off the hook that easily. Wish me luck." Carlita hurried from the apartment, down the steps and into the pawnshop.

Josh stood behind the counter facing a short, red-haired woman who fit Tony's description.

Carlita calmly made her way to the counter. "I'm Carlita Garlucci. How can I help you?"

"I was in here last night right before you closed. I found some items in your store which were stolen from my home a few days ago and a rude man told me I would have to come back today," the woman said haughtily.

Carlita decided to play dumb. "What items?"

"It was a watch, a pair of diamond earrings and a diamond necklace." The woman pointed to the desk. "I watched him put them in an envelope and place them inside the desk drawer."

"How do we know the jewelry belongs to you?" Carlita decided to rattle the woman's cage a little.

It worked. Her face turned beet-red and Carlita thought her red head was going to blow off.

"Because I described two of the items in great detail before I ever saw them," she gritted out.

"If you don't give me my merchandise, I'm going to call the police."

Carlita called her bluff. "I think that's an excellent idea." She reached for her cell phone. "Would you like to call them or shall I?"

She didn't wait for an answer as she scrolled through her list of phone numbers. Unfortunately, she'd had several occasions to contact the police during some recent investigations and the Savannah-Burnham Police Department's number was programmed into her cell phone.

The woman glared at Carlita as she spoke to dispatch and they assured her they would send an officer as soon as possible.

"I'll wait outside." The woman spun on her heel and stomped across the floor, slamming the front door on her way out.

"Whew!" Josh shook his head. "I thought she was going to jump across the counter and attack you."

"She better not, not if she knows what's good for her," Carlita said. She watched the young woman pace back and forth in front of the window as she talked on her cell phone.

Ten minutes later, an officer arrived and the woman hurried over to him. They stood talking for several long moments before they both stepped inside.

Carlita immediately recognized the man. "Detective Polivich."

"Mrs. Garlucci," the detective said. "Ms. Crenshaw briefly explained what happened but I would like to hear your side of the story."

Carlita calmly explained the situation, with several annoying interruptions from the woman.

During the process, Carlita learned the accuser's name was Lyla Crenshaw. She lived not far from the highway in a mobile home park and worked at the Mini Mart convenience store/gas station full-time.

Carlita made a mental note to avoid the Mini Mart and the trailer park.

"This is ridiculous. I clearly identified the items," Lyla interrupted Detective Polivich once again.

The detective abruptly stopped writing and gave her a hard stare. "We can move this process along quicker if you remain silent."

Lyla Crenshaw glared at Polivich but did as she was told.

He turned to Carlita. "Where is the merchandise in question?"

"Here." Carlita pulled the envelope from the drawer and handed it to him. He placed the contents on the desk and took several pictures of the items using his cell phone. When he finished, he dropped the jewelry back inside the envelope and handed it to Carlita.

"What are you doing?" the woman gasped.

"The store will retain possession of the goods in question until the investigation is complete." The detective turned to Carlita. "Please place these in a secure location until we contact you."

"But..." Lyla said, "The jewelry belongs to me."

Detective Polivich lifted a brow. "Ms. Crenshaw, until the investigation is complete, the merchandise remains here."

Lyla stomped her foot in protest. The detective placed his hand under her elbow and led her to the door. "In the meantime, I'm going to ask you to stay away from this establishment until the investigation has been completed."

Carlita smiled.

Mercedes, who had come down right before the detective arrived on scene, stuck her tongue out at the woman's back.

"Mercedes," Carlita admonished.

Detective Polivich and the woman stopped on the sidewalk out front.

"What? The woman is a witch."

"She's upset." Carlita tried to put herself in Lyla Crenshaw's shoes. It was hard, but she tried.

"I'm gonna finish working on the database," Mercedes said. "I should have the information entered in a couple hours and then we can search the list."

"What list is that?" Josh, who had been silent during the entire incident, followed Mercedes to the desk in the corner.

"A list of sellers," Mercedes explained. "We're creating a database so we can track sellers."

Josh studied the computer screen. "I kinda wondered how you kept track of sellers and inventory."

Detective Polivich reentered the store and asked Carlita for the seller's information. She made a copy of Dawson Greene's information and handed the copy to him. "We tried contacting Mr. Greene. We think the information he gave us might be phony."

"I see." The detective studied the sheet, folded it into thirds, slipped it inside his notepad and shoved everything into his pocket.

A customer entered the store. Josh hurried over to greet the shopper while Carlita waved Detective Polivich to the side. "We had another incident early yesterday. It was a similar situation where a customer told us he'd been robbed and the merchandise showed up in our store."

"What happened?"

"We gave him the merchandise and lost money," Carlita said. "At this rate, we'll be out of business in a month."

"You could be a target of a ring of swindlers." The detective rubbed his chin thoughtfully.

"How would it work?" Mercedes asked.

"A ring of thieves robs area homes. One of the thieves, using fake identification, sells the stolen merchandise to an establishment such as yours. The 'victim,' another thief, visits area retailers in 'search' of said merchandise. They find the merchandise in your store. They identify the stolen goods and then start threatening to call local law enforcement or media outlets. You return it and now you, the honest businesswoman, have paid for merchandise and then turned around and handed it back to the thieves."

Carlita's head started to spin. It sounded like an elaborate scheme but the scenario was flawed. "If this is what's happening, why would Ms. Crenshaw be willing to file a police report?" The last thing a criminal would want is contact with local police and for them to open an investigation.

Detective Polivich shifted his feet. "It's just a theory Mrs. Garlucci. We will be investigating the case and plan to look into Ms. Crenshaw's claim." He patted his pocket. "I have your contact information and will let you know as soon as we have anything. In the meantime, please make sure the merchandise is kept in a safe place and not accidentally sold."

"Of course." Carlita walked the detective to the front and followed him out onto the sidewalk.

He turned to go and then turned back. "You sure have had a string of bad luck since moving to Savannah."

Carlita rolled her eyes. "It's like a black cloud following me wherever I go. Sometimes I wonder if I should just move back to New York."

The detective smiled. "I wouldn't go to that extreme. Besides, the streets of Savannah are much safer than the streets of New York City."

Carlita was beginning to wonder.

Chapter 7

Tony returned a short time later and in much better spirits. Carlita and Mercedes told him all that had transpired. He interrupted when Carlita got to the part where Lyla Crenshaw came unglued when Detective Polivich told her she wasn't taking the goods with her. "Man, I would've liked to have seen the look on her face."

Tony took over while Carlita headed upstairs. When she reached the outer hall, her gaze wandered to the apartment in the back. She'd completely forgotten her promise to the potential tenants that she would make a decision that day.

Mercedes had placed a copy of all of the applications in a file folder on the edge of Carlita's desk, a cozy work nook that contained a small file cabinet, Carlita's new laptop and even a set of vertical file holders where she kept the pawnshop paperwork and some of her favorite recipes.

She settled into the desk chair, slipped her reading glasses on and opened the file folder. After scrutinizing each of the applications and reading each of the side notes Mercedes had left for her, she easily decided Charles Benson, aka *Cool Bones* would be her new tenant and neighbor.

She dialed the number listed on his application and left a message for her soon-to-be tenant, letting him know he could move in whenever he wanted, but to call her back to let her know he still wanted the apartment so she could prepare the paperwork and collect the first and last month's rent, plus the security deposit.

Carlita almost called Ben Cutler to tell him she'd selected another tenant but decided to put it off until she had the signed paperwork in hand from Mr. Benson. She was not looking forward to seeing the man again and a shiver ran down her spine. There was something about him…

Tony would be happy she wasn't going to let a government hack as he'd called him, into their building. If Carlita was completely honest with herself, she wasn't keen on having a government agent living under her roof. Elvira was bad enough.

She hoped she wasn't way off on her assessment of Cool Bones, but she didn't think so.

Carlita wandered to the kitchen and grabbed a dishrag to wipe the breadcrumbs Mercedes had missed off the counter. She headed back to the desk and settled in to work on the invitations for the upcoming dinner party.

She started a to-do list, which included asking Mercedes to print the invitations. She jotted down the list of invitees and even added two of the SAS, Savannah Architectural Society, members – Vicki Munroe, the Savannah mayor's sister and her friend, Glenda Fox, along with her husband, Mark.

Carlita had met Mark once, when he and Glenda had stopped by for the grand opening of *Swag in Savannah*. Between area business owners, neighbors and the few friends she had made so far, there were a decent number of invitees.

She logged onto her favorite recipe site, printed off some recipes and then dug through her treasured family recipe box to come up with a tempting array of dishes and desserts.

Mercedes strolled into the apartment, spotted her mother sitting at the desk and wandered over. "Whatcha doing?"

"Working on the dinner menu for Sunday evening's party," Carlita said. "Can you help me print some invitations?"

"Sure. What's the theme?" Mercedes asked.

"Italian."

"Duh. I'll get right on it. I finished entering all the information for the new database." Mercedes headed to her room, but not before promising her mother that she'd pick out some snazzy invitations.

Carlita heard the click of the lock on her door and briefly wondered if her daughter had published the secret book she'd been working on for months now, *Murder, Mayhem and the Mafia, a Mob Daughter's Confessions*. Several times, she'd almost blurted out she knew about the book but stopped short.

She didn't want her daughter to think she was snooping although, technically, it was exactly what she'd done.

Carlita finished jotting down a tentative dinner menu and vowed to work on the grocery list the following day. It would involve a trip to the large super store a few miles away so she wanted to make sure she had a complete list of everything she needed before she talked her daughter into making the drive.

The outer doorbell rang. Carlita sprang from the chair and hustled to the window. She could see the top of a man's head but nothing else.

She hurried to the back door, reminding herself she needed to ask Tony to install a peephole so they could see who was standing on the other side. Carlita unlocked the door and eased it open.

Ben Cutler stood on the other side. He smiled when she opened the door. "Hello Mrs. Garlucci. I hope I'm not bothering you."

"Not at all." Carlita joined him on the stoop and pulled the door shut behind her. "I meant to call you earlier but it has been hectic." She sucked in a deep breath. "I've decided to go with another tenant. I apologize I didn't contact you sooner."

"Wait here and I'll go grab the money you gave me yesterday." Carlita didn't wait for a reply as she sprinted up the steps, stepped into the apartment and retrieved the envelope of money Cutler had given her the previous day.

As she headed back downstairs, she quickly counted the bills to make sure it was all there, although she hadn't touched it since he'd given it to her.

Ben Cutler was standing in the same spot and she handed him the envelope. "I counted it but would like you to do the same, just so we both know it's all there."

The man opened the envelope, pulled out the stack of bills and skimmed through them as he silently counted. "It's all here." He shoved the money back inside the envelope and slipped it into his front pocket. "Was there a problem with my references?"

Carlita shook her head. "I don't think so. To be honest, I let my daughter go over all of the applications and she gave her recommendations after reviewing all of the information. She recommended someone else."

"I see." Ben Cutler rocked back on his heels and studied Carlita.

She had a feeling he didn't believe her, although it was the truth. Mercedes had gone over the applications. The only thing she hadn't shared was that she had already been leaning toward renting to Charles Benson.

"I'm sorry Mr. Cutler. I have a friend, Annie Dowton, who owns Riverfront Real Estate, the real estate office across the street. She may be able to help you find a suitable apartment."

"Thank you. I'll run over there and see if she has anything." Ben Cutler turned to go before turning back. "If your tenant doesn't work out, you have my number."

Before Carlita could answer, he walked down the alley and disappeared around the corner.

Carlita waited until he was out of sight before stepping back inside the building, relieved to have the unpleasant task behind her. As she climbed the stairs, she decided that even if Cool Bones didn't take the apartment, she wasn't going to rent to Ben Cutler. Not now, not ever.

She tidied her desk and checked her cell phone. Cool Bones had left a message so Carlita called him back with the good news. He told her he would be there first thing the following morning to pay and sign the paperwork. He also told her he would move in on Friday.

After she hung up, Carlita realized it was going to be a very busy weekend between moving in a new tenant and hosting a dinner party.

She tapped on Mercedes door. "I'm going to check out the apartment behind us," she hollered through the door.

Rambo decided to tag along and kept her company as she did a thorough walk-through. It was a lovely apartment and she hoped he would enjoy living there. It would be nice to have another male around.

Of course, Tony was in the same building but he was downstairs. Having someone upstairs and closer in the event of an emergency gave Carlita a small inkling of comfort.

Carlita exited the apartment and waited for Rambo to follow her out.

"Well?"

Carlita jumped at the voice behind her. It was Elvira.

"Well what?"

Elvira stuck a hand on her hip. "Did you decide on a new tenant? CB said you showed him the apartment."

"CB. You mean Cool Bones?"

"Yeah. I call him CB for short."

"CB will be here in the morning to sign the lease."

"Sweet," Elvira shrieked. "Hey! I just thought of something...does this mean I get a referral fee?"

Carlita frowned. "A referral fee?"

"You know, like a headhunter, helping you find a quality tenant to rent the apartment."

"I..." She hadn't thought about paying Elvira a dime, but then again, if Charles turned out to be a model tenant and stayed as long as he'd stayed in his current apartment, he might be worth a referral fee. "I suppose. You can take twenty-five dollars off next month's rent."

"Seventy-five," Elvira shot back.

"Fifty," Carlita bartered.

"It's a deal." Elvira held out her hand to shake. "You drive a hard bargain."

She changed the subject. "I saw an unmarked cop car out front earlier. What's going on now?"

The last thing Carlita needed was for Elvira to start poking around in the pawnshop's business.

"Nothing that involves tenants," Carlita said.

"If it's in this building, it involves tenants. Were you robbed? I told you opening a pawnshop would attract a criminal element."

"It wasn't a robbery," Carlita said.

"Stolen goods," Elvira guessed. "You found out you're fencing stolen goods."

Elvira's eyes widened as she studied Carlita's face. "I'm right. You should do a better job of screening your sellers."

Carlita cleared her throat and clenched her fists.

Elvira frowned. "Whatever. Don't let me tell you how to run your business." She reached for her doorknob. "If you get in a pinch, don't forget, you can always hire EC Investigative Services to help you out."

EC Investigative Services was a company Elvira had started after moving into the apartment. Carlita didn't dare ask how business was going. Partly because she didn't want to give Elvira any ideas about snooping around in the Garlucci family's past and partly because she wasn't 100% convinced Elvira's "investigating" techniques were on the up and up.

"I'll keep it in mind." Carlita turned to go. "I'm having a dinner party this Sunday at six o'clock. I'll be serving drinks and appetizers in the courtyard and then moving the dinner portion of the party into this upper hall and my apartment afterward. You're invited, of course."

"What kind of food?" Elvira asked.

Carlita began her mental count to ten before leveling her gaze on her tenant. "Edible food, Elvira. I'm making Chinese. Egg rolls, sushi, lo Mein."

"You're not Chinese. I mean, it's not like you can't serve Chinese food but I would think you being Italian and all, you'd want to serve Italian dishes." Elvira raised both hands. "Not that I don't like Chinese or Italian."

"I was joking," Carlita said. "Of course it will be Italian."

"Good. That makes more sense." Elvira nodded her approval. "I'll be there." She pushed her apartment door open. "Maybe you can invite Cool Bones and his band to play down in the courtyard. They don't take the stage at the Thirsty Crow until nine at night."

"Really?" It was a thought. A good idea, actually, but then, the man hadn't even moved in yet. How could she impose on him before he'd even signed his name on the dotted line?

"I'll ask him," Elvira offered. "I'm going down there tonight to hang out with a few friends, toss down a few beers and listen to some music. Gotta go. I hear my business line ringing." Elvira hurried into her apartment and slammed the door shut behind her.

Carlita wandered back to her apartment. *Elvira had friends?*

Chapter 8

The next morning, Carlita woke early. She had a ton of things on her mind. First and foremost was meeting Charles Benson to sign the paperwork for the apartment and to collect the deposit and rent.

Next on her list was to deliver the invitations for the upcoming party. The previous evening she'd touched base with all of the guests she planned to invite to give them a heads up and then addressed the elegant invitations Mercedes had printed.

Carlita told her daughter they needed to make a trip to the large super store and Mercedes agreed, but told her mother the only way she would go was if Carlita drove them there. She accused her daughter of bribery but Mercedes held her ground.

One way or another, Mercedes was going to get her mother behind the wheel again. Bribery, persuasion, whatever it took.

Carlita poured a cup of coffee and then plopped down at the desk to work on a detailed grocery list.

The appetizer menu included a caprese salad, bruschetta, crusty bread and garlic dip as well as a wine and cheese tray.

For dinner, she planned to make pizzas, her linguine, a spaghetti pie and Italian tacos, foods that would fit on small plates that people could pick up and carry around while they mingled.

She was having a hard time deciding on desserts. Italian cookies would work well but she needed something else.

By the time she finished her menu and grocery list, it was close to ten. Cool Bones would be arriving soon. She grabbed the rental agreement she'd filled out, along with the apartment keys and headed to the alley to wait for him to arrive.

At ten o'clock on the dot, Charles sauntered down the alley, his black felt hat tipped at a jaunty angle, humming a catchy tune.

Carlita smiled when he got close. "Is that one of your songs you were humming?"

Cool Bones smiled wide. "Yes ma'am. I just penned it yesterday and sang it for the first time last night. It's called; *I Signed a Crooked Contract Y'all.*"

"I hope you weren't thinking of the apartment rental agreement when you wrote it."

Cool Bones chuckled. "No ma'am. Just thinkin' 'bout a bad marriage." He waved a hand. "But that's long past. I already done moved on."

"We can't wait to have you." Carlita gave him the tour around the back of the building. Their next stop was the front where she unlocked the courtyard gate and held it open as she waited for him to step inside.

Cool Bones followed her inside and gazed around. "This is a peaceful spot. It will be a welcome respite from my hectic schedule." They wandered to the fountain in the back. He tipped his head back and studied the second story windows. "Are those windows to your unit?"

She shook her head. "My apartment is next to yours. Those windows belong to Elvira on the left and Shelby Townsend, one of my other tenants, on the right. Shelby lives here with her daughter, Violet."

Cool Bones lowered his gaze. "Elvira mentioned something about a party Sunday night."

"Yes. I'm hosting my first dinner party, a cena, and you're invited. It starts at six o'clock here in the courtyard with appetizers. The dinner, more of a light dinner party, will be held in my apartment and in the outer hall. I hope you don't mind and we don't get in the way of you moving in."

"No ma'am. I rented a moving truck and plan to move in Friday," he said. "Elvira mentioned you were going to ask me and my guys if we'd like to play a few songs during the first part of the party."

Carlita's face reddened. Elvira had put her on the spot. "You do not have to do that. It was her suggestion, but not necessary."

"We'd love to," Cool Bones said. "We're always looking for new audiences."

"Well. I've invited Mayor Puckett's sister, Vicki, as well as another member of the Savannah Architectural Society and also some of the Walton Square area business owners."

"Who-ee." Cool Bones let out a low whistle. "It would be our pleasure, Mrs. Garlucci. What time would you like us to set up?"

Carlita quickly ran the timeframe through her head. "Would 5:30 be too early? That way, if guests arrive early, you won't have to maneuver your equipment around them."

"Perfect." Cool Bones rubbed his hands together. "Now where do I sign the good contract y'all?"

They sat at the bistro table inside the courtyard and it took less than five minutes for Charles Benson to sign his name on the dotted line and give her a certified check.

Carlita handed him the keys, explained where the mailbox was located and jotted his mailbox number on the front of his copy of the rental agreement. "There's also a contact list for utility companies and the number for the cable company. The rent includes basic cable but if you would like additional channels, you'll have to pay extra."

Cool Bones thanked her for the information. They chatted for a few more minutes and then headed out of the courtyard. "The keys include a mailbox key, keys to your unit, a key to the entrance door and also a key to the courtyard, which you're free to use anytime you like. Please be sure to lock the gate when you leave."

He promised he would and they slowly made their way to the back of the building. Carlita finally asked the question she'd been dying to ask. "Are you and Elvira close friends?"

Cool Bones stopped in his tracks. "No ma'am. Elvira and some of her friends come by a few times a week when they know I'm playing." He looked around before lowering his voice. "She's been flirtin' with me. You know, layin' it on thick. When she told me about the apartment, I almost didn't bother filling out the application she gave me, especially when I found out it was close to hers."

He raised his voice. "I'm glad I decided to pursue it. I would've missed out on the perfect living arrangement. I bet you got lots of applications."

"Several," Carlita admitted. "You just seemed a perfect fit Charles." They started walking again.

"I would love to come down to the *Thirsty Crow* and listen to you and your band. Do you have a name?"

"Yep. Cool Bones and the Jazz Boys."

When they reached the top of the stairs, they parted ways. "I'm gonna take a look around if you don't mind and then I'll be back early Friday to start movin' in."

"Sounds good." Carlita nodded as she reached for her door handle. "Welcome to Walton Square."

Cool Bones tipped his hat and turned to go.

Elvira's door flew open and she leapt into the hall. "I thought I heard your voice *Charles.*"

Carlita grinned. "Good morning Elvira."

Elvira shot Carlita a quick glance. "Mornin'," she said as she sashayed across the hall. She leaned close to Cool Bones as he stood in front of his apartment door. "When are you moving in?"

Carlita didn't wait for him to answer as she stepped inside her apartment and quietly closed the door behind her. Cool Bones...Charles seemed quite capable of handling Elvira. At least she hoped he was.

The apartment was quiet and Mercedes' bedroom door was still closed. Carlita had heard her daughter rummaging around late last night. She'd never realized Mercedes was such a night owl.

She jotted a note, telling her daughter she was going to walk to the bank to deposit the new tenant's cashier's check and then headed out. Rambo patiently waited by the door and Carlita patted his head. "Sorry Rambo. You can't go to the bank but I'll take you for a walk when I get back," she promised.

The pawnshop had already opened for business and Carlita peeked in the back on her way out. Tony was busy with a customer so she quietly closed the door and stepped into the alley.

A cool morning breeze blew her bangs into her eyes and she swept them off to the side as she gazed up at the sky. Not long after moving to Savannah, Carlita discovered the weather could change in the blink of an eye. She read somewhere it had something to do with living close to the ocean and the ocean breezes.

The bank was several blocks east and not far from the City Market. The bank, like so many other buildings in historic Savannah, was a remarkable piece of history with its towering red brick exterior and black and white striped awnings.

The front door was gold plated and the interior floors were marble tile. The barred grates on the counters reminded Carlita of something out of the movies. She stepped to the first open window.

After depositing the check, she exited the bank but instead of turning right to head back to the apartment, she turned left. Carlita thought about

Ben Cutler, who'd told her he had just taken a job at the IRS office in downtown Savannah. She recalled seeing the impressive building not long after moving to Savannah.

It wasn't far from the bank. She picked up the pace as she strode down the sidewalk. After crossing the street, she continued in the direction of where she thought the building was located. The IRS building was tall but, unlike so many of Savannah's historic district architecture, it was a drab depressing shade of gray.

When she got close to where she remembered seeing it, she slowed her pace. The sign out front was small. If Carlita hadn't been paying attention, she would've missed it. She started to pass by and then stopped. Ben Cutler. There was something about him.

Before she could change her mind, she stepped inside and hurried to the reception desk. The woman behind the desk watched as Carlita approached. "Hello."

"Hello. Yes. I was wondering if Ben Cutler was available."

The woman frowned. "Ben Cutler?" She lowered her gaze and began tapping on the keyboard in front of her. "Can you spell the last name?"

"C-U-T-L-E-R. Ben might be short for Benjamin."

The woman reached for the mouse and scrolled the screen before finally shaking her head. "We have no one here by that name."

Chapter 9

"Are you sure?" Carlita leaned forward.

"Yes ma'am. I typed in Ben Cutler, Benjamin Cutler and I even tried spelling the last name wrong, just in case."

"He's new. Perhaps he's not in your system yet," Carlita said.

"If he's been hired, he would be in our system."

Carlita's mind whirled. "Perhaps he works at a different location."

"I'm not sure about that."

Carlita thanked the woman for the information and slowly retraced her steps. Ben Cutler was not employed at the downtown IRS location. Why did he lie? She remembered the wad of cash he'd given her.

When she got back to the apartment, she made a beeline for the file folder containing the applications. She pulled his from the pile and began scrutinizing it.

Ben Cutler listed Adam Hunt as his supervisor at the IRS. Carlita almost dialed the number listed for Mr. Hunt, but instead tracked down the IRS office she'd just left.

She called the number she found and asked to speak with Adam Hunt. After a brief pause, the man on the other end informed her there was no one there by the name of Adam Hunt.

Carlita was still holding her cell phone when a bleary-eyed Mercedes stumbled out of her room. "Good morning sunshine."

"Ugh. It's way too early to be chipper," Mercedes groaned.

Carlita glanced at the clock sitting on top of the fireplace mantle. "It's almost eleven-thirty in the morning."

"Like I said, it's too early." Mercedes covered her yawn and pulled out a dining room chair. "I couldn't sleep last night. I finished the linguine leftovers."

"That's all right dear. I was going to freeze them." Carlita shifted in her chair. "What is keeping you awake at night?"

Mercedes averted her gaze. "I was thinking about those people who came in, claiming we were selling their stolen goods."

"It's weighing heavy on my mind, too, especially the fact that one of the sellers doesn't exist. I guess we should've done the same thing with the first guy. Held on to the merchandise and called the police to open an investigation."

Mercedes eased into the chair. "I decided since I assembled all the information, I'll take charge of keeping the database up-to-date. Tony has enough to keep him busy. If he can do the wheeling and dealing, I'll handle the paper trail end of it."

"That's a great idea, Mercedes."

"I'm also going to do a little more digging around on my own. I want to look into both the sellers of the supposed stolen merchandise and also the people who claim they were robbed," Mercedes said. "I know the police are investigating, but it wouldn't hurt to look at it ourselves."

"Speaking of which, do you remember Ben Cutler? The applicant who listed the IRS downtown as his employer?"

"Yeah." Mercedes nodded. "He's the guy you didn't like."

"For good reason. I took Mr. Benson's deposit, first and last months' rent to the bank to deposit it this morning. Our bank is not far from the IRS building so I decided to come home that way and on a whim went inside to speak with Mr. Cutler."

Mercedes interrupted. "What did you plan to say?"

"That I had the signed papers on the apartment and to ask if he'd had any luck with Annie Dowton," Carlita said.

"Smart thinking."

"Thanks." Carlita smiled. "Anyway, Mr. Cutler does not work for the Internal Revenue Service."

"Maybe he works at another location."

"It's possible. All I know is there is no Ben or Benjamin Cutler employed by the downtown IRS location." Carlita tapped the top of Cutler's application. "When I got home, I pulled out his application and decided to call back and ask for the person Ben Cutler listed as his supervisor."

"Let me guess," Mercedes said. "His supervisor doesn't work there, either."

"Bingo. I knew there was something about him that didn't sit right. Call it women's intuition, whatever. All I know is Ben Cutler is not who he says he is."

"Good call Ma." Mercedes popped out of her chair and headed to the kitchen where she poured a cup of coffee and stuck it in the microwave to warm it. "After I get ready, I'm going to head down to the pawnshop to enter any new purchases in my new database. I figured it would work best if I updated them on a daily basis to make sure it doesn't get out of control."

Carlita closed Cutler's file and shoved it back inside the file cabinet. "If you keep this up I'll have to give both you and Tony a raise."

They had tentatively decided each of them would collect a salary based on the store's profits, setting aside a percentage for advertising, purchasing inventory, not to mention utilities, taxes and insurance. They hadn't counted on paying for merchandise that had to be returned.

The trio had agreed to give the pawnshop six months to get off the ground and then reassess the business plan. Now that they were generating income from all the apartment units, it would help offset some of the costs.

Because the apartments and pawnshop were technically two separate entities, they decided to run them as two separate businesses.

It was a lot more work at the start up but in the long run things would run more efficiently. This was the reason Tony got a bigger pay percent for the pawnshop since he took the brunt of the work while Carlita took a bigger percentage of the monies coming in from the apartments since she handled that end.

They hadn't had to worry about maintenance or repairs to the units since Carlita had the entire building remodeled prior to moving to Savannah.

Tony wasn't much of a "handyman" so Carlita decided if she needed any work done, she'd hire contractor, Bob Lowman, or one of his workers.

It was one less hassle/headache for Tony to worry about. The pawnshop kept him busy enough.

Mercedes carried her coffee to the bathroom and Carlita could hear her daughter humming as she showered. After she emerged, Carlita reminded her they needed to head to the grocery store to stock up on supplies for the party.

Mercedes took a quick peek at her mother's menu and gave it a nod of approval before heading downstairs to work on her books.

Carlita had gotten so wrapped up in the rental and worrying about her could-have-been tenant, she'd forgotten to eat breakfast, so she munched on a cinnamon bagel and sipped another cup of coffee before heading downstairs.

Melody, one of the new part-time employees, was off to the side, assisting a customer.

Adele was organizing a rack of vintage record albums. Carlita greeted the young woman and headed to the back.

Josh, the other part-timer, and Adele swapped days, every other day, unless one or the other had to switch. Carlita and Tony left it up to them if they needed to make a schedule change, but for the most part, it was one day on and one day off.

Melody had only started a couple days ago and Tony was still training her.

Within the month, they would have to make a decision about which one to offer more hours. Tony was their main contact for issues, but Carlita had worked around both Josh and Adele, and felt they were equally competent and hard working.

Carlita secretly thought Tony favored Josh over Adele. According to Tony, the young man had had a few brushes with the law. His pierced lip and the big round disc in his ear had caused Carlita to pause but Tony had convinced his mother to give him a chance. She was glad she had.

After Tony explained he'd come from a rough side of town and gotten involved with the wrong crowd but was trying to clean up his act, she knew her son was right.

Adele, on the other hand, was much quieter. Carlita knew little about her other than she lived in Rollins Square in a small apartment with her grandfather.

Carlita didn't want to pry into her personal life so she didn't know much more than that, other than she'd dropped out of high school in the eleventh grade and had finished her high school education on line.

While Adele worked on the other side of the room, Tony and Mercedes stood hovering near the desk, talking in low voices. Carlita wandered over. "How's it going?"

"It's not." Mercedes frowned. "All the entries I put in yesterday. Pfft. Gone!" She snapped her fingers.

"What do you mean they're gone?"

"The file is missing."

Tony lifted his hands. "I swear. I didn't touch it. I have no idea what happened."

Mercedes grabbed a sheet of paper off the desk and headed to the printer. "Thank goodness I decided to email a copy of the file to my personal email. I'm printing off a copy, just in case."

She plucked the papers from the printer. "I'm going to start matching inventory now, just to make sure everything is accounted for."

"You don't trust me?" Tony growled.

Carlita patted her son's arm. "Of course she trusts you. It's just a precautionary measure."

"Chillax bro." Mercedes eased past her brother and headed for the first display case. She opened the case and pulled out a tray of earrings. "We're only going to get busier so the more efficient and streamlined we are, the better off we'll be."

Tony shot his sister a dark look.

Carlita thought she was going to have to referee but thankfully, a seller entered the store carrying a large box of items.

Tony crossed the store to greet the seller while Carlita wandered over to chat with Melody. She thought about inviting Melody to the party but decided to leave it up to Tony since she'd only met her one time. The young woman was pleasant but seemed distracted so Carlita kept the conversation brief.

She headed upstairs to grab Melody, Adele and Josh's invitations from the stack and returned to the store.

Adele was helping a customer and she waited for her to finish.

While she waited, a familiar male voice caught her attention. She peered around the corner of a center column and to where Tony stood discussing some merchandise.

She took a second long look at the man and realized it was none other than Ben Cutler. He caught her eye at the same time she realized who he was and her heart skipped a beat.

"Hello Mrs. Garlucci."

"Mr. Cutler. What a surprise."

"I wanted to stop by to thank you for recommending Annie Dowton and to let you know right after I left here the other day I found an apartment two squares over."

"I'm glad to hear it." Carlita pointed at the box of merchandise. "Cleaning house before you move?"

"Yes, as a matter of fact," Cutler, if that was his real name, said. "The less I have to move, the better."

"I see." Carlita stepped closer. "How is your new job at the IRS office working out?"

Ben Cutler rocked back on his heels and studied her face. "Great. I love my new office. Savannah is such a fascinating area, full of rich history with so much to explore."

"I agree. It's a great area," she said. "Nothing like Queens, New York. I can't recall if you ever told me where you moved here from."

"Chicago. The north side of Chicago," he said. "I grew tired of the cold, gloomy winters."

"This will be my first winter in the south as well. Did you bring family with you?"

"No," Cutler said. "I'm a single man. Never married, no children."

A slow smile spread across his face. "I believe I noted on my application I would be the only one moving into your unit."

"My memory isn't what it used to be." Carlita pointed to the box. "Thank you for thinking of us. Good luck on your new home."

Carlita excused herself and wandered to the corner desk where Adele sat, sorting through a stack of coins. She leaned forward and whispered in her ear. "The man that Tony is talking to...have you ever seen him before?"

Adele casually turned to face Carlita and peered over her shoulder as she studied Ben Cutler. "No. He doesn't look familiar."

"I won't go into details, but please take a good look at his face and if you ever see him inside the store again, please let me know."

"Absolutely." Adele nodded solemnly. "I got a good look at his face."

Carlita sifted through the invitations and pulled Adele's out. "I'm having a party Sunday evening. You're invited. It starts at six o'clock."

Adele took the invitation. "Thanks. I'll let you know."

Carlita patted the young woman's arm and turned her attention to the bag sitting on the desk. "What are you doing?"

"Someone just sold us a trench coat. There was a small bag in one of the pockets." Adele picked up a coin. "It was full of coins and Tony wanted me to sort through them to see if any looked old or valuable. So far there are just a bunch of dirty pennies."

She turned her hand over to reveal a layer of grit on her fingertips. "It's a dirty job but somebody's got to do it."

"Looks like fun. I'll let you get back to work." She patted Adele's arm and stepped over to Mercedes who was studying a sheet of paper, a deep frown etched on her face.

"How is it going?"

"It's not." Mercedes looked up. "The code I have for this piece of jewelry does not match up to what's in the system." She set the gem-studded broach on the counter and picked up a stone-encrusted egg. "This isn't even in the system." She turned it over. "There's no tag."

Chapter 10

"We have another problem." Carlita grabbed a slip of paper and began writing furiously. '*The man talking to Tony and trying to sell his stuff is Ben Cutler.*'

Mercedes' eyes widened and she glanced at her brother and Cutler. She took the pen from her mother. '*I...have an idea.*'

"Watch the counter," she whispered. Carlita's daughter strolled over to the men and casually propped her elbow on the counter as she listened to Tony haggle with Ben Cutler. She pulled the box toward her and then reached inside, pulling out a set of headphones. "This looks like something we might be interested in."

Melody walked over. "Do you mind if I take a quick lunch break?"

"Sure. Sorry Melody. I lost track of time," Tony apologized.

"No problem." She waved a hand. "I'll be back in a few." The employee walked out the front door and passed by the front picture window.

"We're not interested in the headphones." Tony gave his sister a dark look.

Mercedes shrugged and handed the headphones to Cutler. "You're the expert."

Tony opened his mouth to speak and quickly clamped it shut. "I'll go get the cash for the car speakers, the metal detector and the leather jacket." He gave his sister a hard stare and walked to the back, returning moments later with a stack of bills. He counted the money into Ben Cutler's open hand.

Cutler shoved the money in his front pocket and picked up his box. "Thanks."

After he exited the store, Tony turned to his sister. "What's the 411?"

"That was Ben Cutler," Mercedes said.

"Yeah. I got the guys' info right here. So what?"

"Ben Cutler," Carlita said. "The man who wanted to rent the apartment and paid in cash. The same man who made me uncomfortable."

"Yeah? So he's got goods to sell," Tony said.

"Let's see where he's going." Mercedes grabbed her mother's arm and darted out the front door and onto the sidewalk. "I think he went this way." They hurried around the corner and Carlita caught a glimpse of his tall, dark head.

"He's heading downtown."

"Let's follow him," Carlita said impulsively.

Mercedes stopped abruptly at the corner. "This way." They picked up the pace and jogged to the end of the block.

"He's moving fast," Mercedes said breathlessly. "We'll have to pick up the pace."

"Good thing I'm wearing my flats," Carlita groaned, the heels of her shoes slapping the pavement. Several pedestrians gave them odd stares as they ran down the sidewalk. "I hope he stops soon."

They ran three full city blocks. All the while, Mercedes kept one eye on Cutler and one eye on the maze of pedestrians. "He slowed down."

"Thank goodness." Carlita slowed her pace and fought to catch her breath. "I'm out of shape."

"He stopped," Mercedes reported.

Carlita squinted her eyes and peered down the sidewalk. "I don't see him anymore."

"He must've gone inside a building. The good news is I think I know where we lost his trail."

The women continued walking. "I wonder if the *Thirsty Crow* is in this area."

Mercedes shifted her gaze. "Yeah. It's down here. I've seen it."

"Cool Bones, our new tenant, works there. I told him we'd come by and listen to him and his band, the Jazz Boys, play. Which reminds me, he and his band are going to play out in the courtyard for the first part of our dinner party this Sunday evening."

"Cool." Mercedes pointed at a building up ahead and across the street. "There's the *Thirsty Crow*. Do you want to check it out?" Mercedes asked.

"Maybe later," Carlita said. "For now, I would like to figure out where we lost Ben Cutler's trail."

They reached the designated spot and Carlita slipped into the shadow of a nearby doorway. "I hope he doesn't catch us following him."

"I think it was the building next door." Mercedes joined her mother in the doorway.

Carlita leaned forward and peered down the sidewalk, but for the life of her couldn't tell what the building was. There was no name on the front. The exterior blended in with several others on the block.

"There's only one way to find out what it is. We'll have to take our chances." Carlita tugged on her daughter's arm and the two of them began a brisk walk toward the building.

When they got close, Carlita spotted a name etched in the stonework on the front of the building. *E.L. Ivey.*

Mercedes reached into her back pocket and pulled out her cell phone. She turned it on and held it up.

"What are you doing?" Carlita whispered.

"I'm taking a picture so I can research this later."

"Oh. Good idea."

Mercedes shoved her phone back inside her pocket. "If this is where Cutler lives, he's got a sweet location, right near all the bars and clubs, not to mention across from the river."

"Our place is boring and quiet, huh." Carlita worried her daughter wasn't meeting enough people her own age. The only person she ever spent time with was Autumn and lately it seemed as if Autumn was too busy to hang out. "Maybe you should join a writer's club or book club."

The words escaped Carlita's mouth before she could stop them.

"That's not a bad idea. I love reading. Maybe I can connect with other readers."

And writers. Carlita silently added. "There's a book store not far from our place. I saw it not long ago."

"It's a thought. Maybe I should go check it out. In my free time, of course," Mercedes added.

"Of course." The women headed back toward the apartment.

"I'm hungry," Mercedes said.

"Let's order pizza. We can eat it for lunch and save the leftovers for dinner."

When they reached the apartment, Carlita headed upstairs to order the food while Mercedes resumed her task of inventorying the pawnshop merchandise.

It was a tedious task and Carlita was glad her daughter was doing it and not her.

After the pizza arrived and they ate, Carlita grabbed her stack of invitations, stopping by the pawnshop to let Tony know she was taking Rambo for a walk and to pass out the party invites.

She stopped by the Parrot House to deliver Pirate Pete's invitation first. He wasn't there so Carlita left it with the hostess.

Next on her list were the Walton Square business owners including the Fischers, the Colbys, Steve and Autumn as well as Annie and Cindy. John Alder didn't answer his front door when she knocked. She could hear muffled pounding coming from inside so she slipped the invitation into the mail slot and kept going.

Her last stop was the Savannah Architectural Society. She smiled as she stopped abruptly in front of the entrance door. The building was narrow, which may have been a major understatement.

Carlita was certain if she stood at the center of the building and extended both arms, she would easily be able to touch both front corners.

The bright red entrance door was tall and thin, a perfect match for the structure. It made the building look even narrower since it covered half the front. On both sides of the door were tall narrow windows.

She started to open the door and then paused. She hoped Betty Graybill, the President of the SAS, was not there. Carlita and Betty had started off on the wrong foot and stayed there.

She let out the breath she'd been holding when she stepped inside and spotted her friend,

Glenda Fox, as well as Vicki Munroe, the two people she'd planned to invite to the party.

Elvira had taken a job with the SAS, right before moving into her apartment and she'd given Carlita a hard time about opening her pawnshop. The miniscule amount of power Elvira held as a member of the SAS had gone right to the woman's head, at least that's what Carlita thought.

"Well. What a pleasant surprise." Glenda slid out of her chair and met her friend at the door. She hugged Carlita.

"I have your invitation for the dinner party I'm hosting Sunday evening." Carlita handed Glenda her invitation. "I hope you and Mark can make it."

She stepped over to Vicki's desk. "I have one for you and a guest, as well."

Vicki swiveled in her chair. "Oh. I got your voice mail message the other night. I just love parties." She flipped the envelope over and slid the invitation out. "Sunday night. I'll be there. My sister is in town visiting. Do you mind if she tags along?"

"The more the merrier." Carlita beamed. "The theme is Italian, of course. I'll be serving appetizers in the courtyard and we'll even have live music. My new tenant, Charles Benson and his band, the Jazz Boys, will be playing out in the courtyard starting at 6:00. Afterward, we'll move upstairs for the meal and mingle."

Vicki looked up from the invitation. "You said Charles Benson and the Jazz Boys are playing? They're very talented."

"Yes. I haven't heard them yet," Carlita admitted. "Elvira hangs out at the *Thirsty Crow* where they play."

Glenda changed the subject. "How is Elvira these days?"

"You haven't seen her?" Carlita assumed all SAS members were required to show up at the office, at least every once in a while.

"No. Elvira quit two weeks ago."

Chapter 11

Carlita's mouth fell open. "She quit?"

"Yep." Glenda nodded. "She waltzed in here one day, packed up her things and told us she was embarking on a new career."

Vicki chuckled. "According to Elvira she found her 'life's calling.'"

"Elvira's private investigative business must have really taken off," Carlita said.

"She's a PI? How fitting," Glenda said. "She was always in here, nosing around in stuff she shouldn't have."

"That's sounds about right," Carlita said. "As long as she can pay her rent and behaves herself, I don't care if she's runs a trolley tour."

The girls thanked her again for the invitation and Carlita stepped out onto the sidewalk. There was a spring in her step as she strolled home. The dinner party would be a fun event and something she should have done months ago.

She hoped when she was ready to start working on the restaurant she wouldn't have to jump through as many hoops and deal with the drama she'd experienced since moving to Savannah.

Carlita thought when she moved from Queens to Savannah, it would be a much more laid back, slower pace of living. So far, it had been the exact opposite.

Mercedes was sitting at Carlita's desk working on her computer when she arrived home. She dropped her keys on the hook and eyed her daughter with interest. "Did something happen to your laptop?"

"No." Mercedes hopped out of the chair. "I finished the first half of my inventory downstairs. There are several items not inventoried correctly. I brought them up here so Tony doesn't accidentally sell them before I have time to clear up the discrepancies."

"What kinds of items?" Carlita asked.

"There's a watch, a woman's diamond tennis bracelet and this." Mercedes reached into a bag propped up against the file cabinet and pulled out the gem-encrusted egg she'd been researching earlier.

Carlita picked up the egg and gently turned it over in her hand. "This looks like it might be worth something."

"I think so, too. I plan to do a little research," Mercedes said. "Maybe Tony didn't tag it because he wasn't sure what it was worth."

Carlita handed it back to her daughter. "I wonder how much he paid for it."

"I have no idea." Mercedes set the egg on top of the desk. "I have some other things to work on in my room. What time do you want to head out the grocery store tomorrow morning?"

"The sooner the better." Carlita wanted plenty of time to prep for the party. She'd hoped for everyone to give verbal RSVPs soon. Annie and Cindy already said they were coming. So were Steve, Autumn, the Colby's, Vicki Munroe, John Alder and Elvira.

The only 'maybes' were Shelby, Glenda and her husband, Pirate Pete, Melody, Josh and Adele.

She decided to shop as if all were going to attend and even if she had leftovers, she could send food home and freeze the rest.

Mother and daughter agreed to leave at ten the next morning and then Mercedes headed to her room, carrying the delicate egg.

Carlita spent the rest of her day on Pinterest researching party ideas and jotting notes on her ever-growing shopping list. She felt as if she hit the jackpot when stumbled on a website listing the most popular southern dishes.

There was an entire section devoted to desserts. She read with interest one of the top five desserts was hummingbird cake. According to the article, it was one of the most requested recipes on *Southern Dining*, the online monthly magazine she'd found.

The ingredients – crushed pineapple, walnuts and bananas, not to mention cream cheese frosting - sounded delicious. The author mentioned many southerners believed hummingbird cake brought good luck for an entire year to anyone who ate a piece. "I need all the help I can get." Carlita added the ingredients to her shopping list and then printed off the recipe.

As she perused the list of invitees and then studied the grocery list, she worried the party would be a flop. Vinnie had never been keen on parties so they rarely hosted one, except for immediate family. Now that she thought about it, they rarely attended parties.

Looking back, she realized her husband was trying to shield his wife and daughter from some of the criminal elements he surrounded himself with. She sometimes wondered if he regretted becoming involved in the mafia. Near the end of his life, he must have, especially when he made his wife promise on his deathbed she would get their sons out of the business.

After munching on leftover pizza, Carlita wrapped a few slices in plastic wrap and carried them downstairs for Tony, who was waiting on customers inside the pawnshop. The days were growing shorter and they had discussed changing their hours of operation since they didn't get many walk-ins after dark.

Carlita was all for closing the store early, especially if Tony was running it by himself. He didn't seem concerned to be working alone after dark and on more than one occasion insisted his Smith & Wesson was all he needed.

She waited until the customers, who were eyeing an Xbox and stack of games for their children, finally decided to buy the items and then exited the store.

Tony followed them out and locked the door behind them before turning the sign to *Closed*.

"I brought you some pizza."

Tony zigzagged past a rack of jackets and met his mother in the back. "Thanks Ma. Shelby invited me over for a late dinner."

"Ah." Carlita lifted a brow. "I stuck her invitation to Sunday's dinner party under her door."

"I'll find out if she's going to be able to make it."

Carlita briefly told her son of the party plans and how the new tenant had offered to play in the courtyard. She also told him about her conversation with Glenda and that Elvira had quit her job.

"So she has the hots for our new tenant." Tony laughed. "At least the heat's off me now. Poor guy. Mercedes told me you ran into a dead end trying to follow the Cutler guy earlier."

"Yeah. We tracked him as far as a building close to the river and then the trail dropped off. We think he went into one of the buildings and Mercedes took a picture of the building so she could do some research." Carlita tugged on a stray strand of hair. "I still think he lied to us."

Tony reached for the pizza, removed the plastic wrap and took a bite. "People have reasons for hiding stuff. Look at us."

"True." If Walton Square neighbors knew half their family secrets, they would run them out of town. "I haven't heard back from Detective Polivich." She told her son how Mercedes and she were going to shop for the party in the morning and then take a drive by the addresses of the sellers whose merchandise was reported as stolen.

Tony took another bite of pizza and chewed thoughtfully. "I'm beginnin' to question myself. Mercedes found a few items I either forgot to tag or the tags were wrong."

"Don't be too hard on yourself, son. Shame on me for dumping everything on your plate. I think it's a good idea for Mercedes and even me to help with the paperwork. You have enough to worry about."

The doorknob rattled, followed by a light tap. Tony turned to face the store window, shook his head and mouthed the words "we're closed" as he pointed at the sign.

"I better head upstairs. Shelby is making steak fajitas."

Carlita pointed at the half-eaten slice of pizza. "I hope you're still hungry."

"This? This is just a snack." She led the way and Tony followed her out of the store, but not before pulling the blinds closed. They'd decided to install vertical blinds to discourage "after hours" non-paying shoppers from casing the joint and potentially breaking into the pawnshop to rob it.

Carlita never would've thought to install the blinds but Tony, much more street-savvy than his mother and sister, was all over it.

Mother and son parted ways at the top of the stairs but not before Carlita reminded her son to mention the party to Shelby. The closer Carlita could get to a head count, the better off she would be.

She hoped Shelby could make it to the party. If not, she was concerned the noise from the outer hall would disturb the mother and daughter although she planned to wrap up the festivities at a decent hour.

Mercedes spent the rest of the evening holed up in her room while Carlita curled up on the couch with Rambo and Grayvie to watch some television. She'd recently gotten hooked on a series called *Secrets of Our Lives*. The series was about couples where one of the spouses led a secret, double life. It sounded a lot like Vinnie and her.

Finally, her daughter emerged from her room and headed to the kitchen to grab a snack.

Carlita set the remote on the coffee table and waited until she finished rummaging around in the kitchen.

"Are you still researching the egg?"

"Nope." Mercedes shuffled into the living room, sank into the recliner and tore off a chunk of her breadstick. "I'm working on something else."

"Another book?" The words flew from Carlita's mouth before she could stop them.

Mercedes nearly dropped the breadstick. "W-what book?"

It was too late for Carlita to backtrack now. "The mafia story." Carlita lifted Grayvie from her lap and set him on the floor before turning to her daughter. "I saw a copy a long time ago, when we were still living in New York," she said softly.

"You...did?" Mercedes was flabbergasted. "I didn't think anyone knew. Anyone except my readers."

"You published the book?"

Mercedes crammed the rest of the breadstick in her mouth and popped out of the chair. "I'll show you." She darted from the room, returning moments later carrying her laptop. She settled in next to her mother and tilted the screen so they both could see. "Check it out."

Carlita fumbled for her reading glasses. Her eyes scanned the screen. "Where is it?"

Mercedes pointed. "There."

Sure enough, *Murder, Mayhem and the Mafia, a Mob Daughter's Confession* was at the top of the screen. "What do you think of the cover?" Mercedes tapped the keyboard to enlarge the picture.

"I...uh." Carlita stared at the bloody scene, a man sprawled out on the pavement, lying in a pool of bright red blood. Off in the distance was a police car, parked in the middle of the road. A large yellow moon hung low over a city skyline. "It's bloody," she blurted out.

"It's a crime scene," Mercedes patiently explained. "The cover is the most violent part of the book. The inside isn't nearly as graphic as the cover."

"Have you gotten any reviews?" Carlita asked.

"A couple." Mercedes wrinkled her nose. "One reader said it wasn't gritty enough and another commented I didn't know anything about the mob."

"If they only knew."

"Right?" Mercedes rolled her eyes. "I started working on a sequel but I'm only selling a couple books a day. How do authors make any money from writing books? I would have to start robbing banks if I had to live off my sales."

"I don't know, Mercedes," Carlita shook her head. "Don't give up on your first attempt. Finish the second book. In the meantime, join a writer's group or try what I suggested, head down to the bookstore around the corner. Maybe someone who works there knows some of the other local authors you can connect with."

"Yeah." Mercedes exited the screen and shut the lid on her laptop. "I guess I will since I've already put so much time and effort into it."

"It's like riding a bike," Carlita said. "The more you practice, the better you'll get, although I'm sure it's awesome."

"Do you want to read it?" Mercedes excitedly flipped the lid back up.

"Of course. How do I buy it? Not an online copy but one I can hold in my hands." She gave her daughter a quick hug. "I'm so proud of you. How many people can say they're a published author?"

Mercedes helped her mother purchase a copy of her book and then headed off to bed. Carlita waited until she disappeared inside her room before scooching off the couch and shuffling to the kitchen for a glass of water.

Rambo followed behind. "Oh no. I almost forgot. Do you want to go out before we settle in for the night?"

Rambo wagged his tail, a definite yes and the two made their way into the alley. Carlita had had Bob Lowman install a hall light as well as a motion detector light above the back door.

It flickered on when they reached the alley and Carlita looked both ways before Rambo and she quietly walked toward the grassy area of the parking lot. The dark alley, full of shadows, sometimes creeped her out when she walked Rambo late at night.

The adjacent building was for sale and currently vacant. There were times Carlita could swear someone was watching her. She shivered as the sensation of being watched and eyed the back of the building nervously.

Boom! The sound of a dumpster lid banging shut caused Carlita to jump. She tightened her grip on Rambo's leash. "Let's hurry," she urged the pooch as they picked up the pace.

A large mercury light illuminated the parking lot, which should have made Carlita feel a little more at ease but instead, made her feel like she was standing in a spotlight. She wandered off to the side and into the shadows.

After Rambo finished his business, Carlita and he began a quick trot back to the building. They were halfway home when the lights from the upper empty apartment behind hers flickered.

"What in the world?" Carlita stared at the windows. There was no way Cool Bones would be inside the empty apartment late at night. It had to be someone else.

Chapter 12

Carlita quietly eased the alley door open and tiptoed up the stairs. Rambo's nails clicked on the wooden steps as they made their way to the top and she inwardly cringed, hoping the sound wouldn't give them away.

She stayed close to the wall in an attempt to avoid the creaky center floorboards as she passed by her apartment door and made her way to the apartment behind hers.

The empty apartment door was ajar and a small ray of light streamed into the upper hall. Carlita could hear the faint echo of footsteps on the wooden floor.

She glanced behind her, deciding the wisest thing to do was to ask her son to go with her to investigate but Rambo blew their cover when he let out an unexpected growl followed by a loud bark.

The door flew open and Elvira stuck her head into the hall. "Good grief! That dang dog of yours scared the crap out of me."

Carlita's eyes widened as she stared at her pain-in-the-rear tenant. "Scared the crap out of you? What are *you* doing in Charles Benson's apartment? But before you answer that, *how* did you get into his apartment?"

"I picked the lock." Elvira reached inside her pocket and pulled out a small flat tool. On one end was a curved hook. "You should have the locks changed. As soon as I realized I could pick the locks on all of these apartment doors, I replaced mine."

"Replaced the lock?" Carlita exploded. "You need permission to change your locks." Technically, it had never stopped Elvira before. She'd painted her apartment walls, not to mention spray painting the courtyard walls, trimming a tree she insisted was blocking her view into the courtyard and now she was changing locks.

Carlita began to mentally count backward from ten as she closed her eyes. "I'll need a key to your apartment."

"Why?" Elvira asked.

Carlita's eyes flew open. "In case something happens and I need to get in there," she gritted between clenched teeth as her blood pressure began to rise.

"I don't have a spare key," Elvira said coolly. "If you insist on having a key, you'll have to give me some money to buy one."

"Are you low on funds since you quit your job at the SAS?"

It was Elvira's turn to look surprised. "Who told you that?"

"It doesn't matter," Carlita said. "In fact, I could care less as long as you pay your rent.

Snooping into other people's business must be a lucrative career these days." She nudged her foot against the apartment door and pushed it all the way open. "Speaking of snooping, you haven't explained to me what you were doing in Mr. Benson's apartment."

"I'm taking some measurements." Elvira pulled a small tape measure from her front pocket. "I painted a portrait of Cool Bones. I've been working on it for a while."

She hurried into the empty apartment and paused in front of the living room fireplace. Carlita trailed behind.

A small mound of plaster covered one of the slate stones in front of the fireplace. A large, gold hook protruded from the wall above the fireplace.

"Since you're here, you can help me hang it. It's kind of heavy. Between the two of us we should be able to carry it over without damaging the edges of the frame."

Elvira darted out of the apartment.

"I can't wait to see it," Carlita muttered as she followed Elvira across the hall and into her apartment.

"Here it is." Elvira pointed at a painting propped against the living room wall.

Carlita's eye narrowed as she studied the painting. She had to admit it was pretty good. Elvira had managed to capture the twinkle in Cool Bones' eyes, the laugh lines near the corners of his mouth and even the jaunty angle of his felt hat.

Behind him were several other men. Carlita knelt down to study the scene. To the right of Cool Bones was a saxophone player, a man playing a trombone and another playing the trumpet.

To the left was a man playing guitar and another on drums. The final person in the portrait was a blonde-haired woman. She was playing piano. "Are those the Jazz Boys?" Carlita asked.

"Yep." Elvira nodded. "At least it *was* the Jazz Boys, until they added the tramp playing the piano."

"Tramp?" Carlita gazed at the woman and realized the woman was scowling while the other band members were smiling.

"She flirts with all the band members and CB in particular," Elvira said. "I think that's how she got the job. I told Smooth Sully, their old piano player, to stick with the Jazz Boys because I was certain they were on the edge of a big break but he wouldn't listen."

Elvira placed her hand on her hip. "He up and quit and now he's playing with the River Rats over at the Black Stallion Club in the riverfront district. I tried to warn Sully I heard rumors the River Rats had mafia ties but he wouldn't listen."

Carlita's breath caught in her throat as she waited for Elvira to elaborate but she changed the subject instead. "So what do you think of the portrait?"

"You did a good job capturing Cool Bones' look, although his band members' faces are blurry."

"Of course they are," Elvira said. "Cool Bones is the star. He should be in the spotlight. The others are just..." She waved her hand dismissively.

"Eye candy," Carlita teased.

"Eye candy?" Elvira sputtered. "Not even close. No one holds a candle to Cool Bones."

Carlita chuckled. Poor Cool Bones. Elvira obviously had a major crush on the man. She noticed a second painting propped next to Cool Bones. It was a woman sitting atop a Harley-Davidson. Her black hair was spiked and stood straight out from her head. In the background was a blur of green. "Who is this?"

"My sister, Dernice," Elvira said. "I thought she was coming to Savannah to visit me for her birthday. She got a little sidetracked."

"Ah." Carlita remembered Elvira mentioning her sister, who lived in California. She was a biker chick. "Didn't you tell me she was in the slammer?"

"Yep." Elvira nodded. "She got in with the wrong crowd and ended up in prison for armed robbery. She's out now and just recently got permission to leave the state."

She grabbed the top of the painting and slid it forward. "She's headed our way, riding her motorcycle, but I have no idea when she's gonna get here. Last I heard, her bike broke down in Oklahoma. A group of nudists from a nearby nudist colony helped her get it fixed."

Elvira shook her head. "Her new buds talked her into hanging around for a while. She's decided to give the carefree, clothing-free lifestyle a try. I may never hear from her again."

Visions of an older, naked Elvira flashed through Carlita's mind and she mentally shook the image. "I can't wait to meet her," she said and quickly changed the subject. "Would you like me to help you carry Cool Bones across the hall?"

"Yes."

Carlita carefully lifted one side of the painting while Elvira lifted the other. The women slowly shuffled across the hall and into the empty apartment. They eased the portrait against the front of the fireplace.

"I have a ladder." Elvira returned moments later carrying a small utility ladder. She set it in front of the fireplace.

The women gingerly lifted the painting and slid it onto the mantle. It took several attempts to slip the wire onto the wall hook before they were finally able to secure the painting.

Carlita stepped to the center of the room to help Elvira straighten the portrait. She gave her a thumbs up. "Perfect."

She could see that the woman had put a lot of time and effort into the painting and Carlita hoped her new tenant would appreciate it. He seemed like a nice man.

"That's a thoughtful housewarming gift," Carlita said.

She could've sworn Elvira's cheeks turn a tinge of pink. "I hope so. He said he was moving in Friday and offered to play out in the courtyard for the party."

"He did. Thank you for putting the bug in his ear."

"You're welcome." The women stepped into the hall and Carlita waited until Rambo joined them before shutting off the apartment lights, and closing and locking the door behind them.

Elvira took a step toward her apartment and then stopped. "You really should consider changing the locks on your door or at the very least, installing a heavy-duty deadbolt." She didn't wait for Carlita to answer as she slipped inside her apartment and closed the door.

Carlita shook her head as she made her way to her apartment. If there was one thing she knew about her tenant it was that she never knew what the woman would do next.

***

"I am not driving," Mercedes insisted. She reached for the GPS, suctioned to the car's dashboard. "I'm putting these addresses in the GPS while you drive."

"Don't blame me if we end up dead," Carlita said dramatically as she glanced in her side mirror, praying she wouldn't sideswipe Tony's car which was parked next to hers.

Mercedes chuckled. "If we're dead it won't matter, will it?"

"That's not the point." Carlita finished backing the car and then shifted into drive. She crept to the end of the alley and turned her blinker on. "We're turning right, right?"

"Right." Mercedes grinned. "When you get to the stop sign, take another right. Taylor Street will take us all the way to the highway."

"The highway?" Carlita's heart pounded. "You expect me to drive on the highway?"

"Yes. Highway driving is easier than city driving. You'll have to be careful when we merge into traffic."

"It's all coming back to me now." She remembered when Mercedes was practicing driving and they nearly collided with another vehicle when her daughter attempted to merge onto the highway. "Maybe I should cancel the party and turn around and go home."

"Ma," Mercedes said. "You're going to cancel a party you're looking forward to just because you're afraid to drive on the highway?"

"No. I'm not afraid to drive on the highway. I'm afraid to drive anywhere." Carlita pressed on the gas and the car picked up some speed as they drove out of the downtown area and onto the four-lane road leading to I-95. Despite being terrified and clenching the steering wheel in a 9:00 o'clock and 3:00 o'clock death grip, she had to admit the road wasn't nearly as congested as downtown Savannah and less cars meant less to have to watch out for.

She loosened her grip on the steering wheel and gave her daughter, who was still fiddling with the GPS, a quick glance. "While we're out, we need to pick up a set of locks for our apartment door."

"The locks are new. Why would we want to replace them already?"

"Because Elvira picked the lock on the unit behind us and she said it was a piece of cake."

"Oh my goodness." Mercedes set the GPS in her lap. "Does this mean she's been sneaking into our apartment when we're not home?"

"I hope not." Carlita hadn't thought of that. With Elvira, anything was possible. "We're definitely getting new locks. What about one of those touchpad, combo locks? Do you think she could crack into one of those?"

"We'll ask when we stop at the hardware store." Mercedes pressed the base of the GPS on the suction cup holder and leaned back. "We're almost there." She finished giving her mother directions to the grocery store.

Carlita crept into the large parking lot and parked way in the back, in an area where she could drive through instead of having to back up again.

Mercedes unlocked her seatbelt. "Chicken Little."

"At least we made it in one piece," Carlita argued.

"True. You're doing much better today."

The women made quick work of finding everything on Carlita's detailed list. When they discovered there was a whole section of household items including hardware store merchandise, they perused the door lock shelves and decided to pick up a couple different kinds. The more the better was Carlita's motto.

After checking out, they loaded the overflowing cartful of groceries into the trunk. Carlita shut the trunk and attempted to hand her daughter the car keys.

Mercedes took a step back. "Oh no. This driving practice is round trip. You have to get us back home."

"Mercedes," Carlita pleaded but her daughter wouldn't budge.

"You're doing great. Besides, I need to scope the places out when we drive by."

"I almost forgot. Where are we going?"

"To check out the addresses of the sellers who supposedly sold us the fenced goods. I also found a couple items and sellers with different names but the same address. One of the addresses sounds familiar."

"Familiar as in we know who it is? Carlita slid behind the wheel, closed the driver's side door and stuck the key in the ignition.

"You'll see when we get there," Mercedes said mysteriously.

"I hope it's not too far out of the way," Carlita said. "We have dairy and frozen stuff that needs to be refrigerated."

"The addresses are all in the same area and on the way." Mercedes reached for her seatbelt. "I mapped the whole route. It will be an extra ten minutes of drive time, tops."

The drive back was less nerve-wracking than the drive to the store. There was only one minor incident where Carlita almost sideswiped a car she didn't see while trying to move into the right lane to exit the highway.

The GPS led them to the north end of downtown Savannah and an area Carlita had never visited before. It was a quiet neighborhood. Lining both sides of the street were tidy ranch homes, situated close together with postage stamp sized yards.

Carlita slowed the car when they got close to the first location. She kept one eye on the road as she zigzagged around several cars parked on the sides of the street. "Well?"

"Nothing here," Mercedes said. "I don't see anything that looks suspicious. Let's head to the next location."

The second address Mercedes wanted to check out was only a couple blocks from the first one. All of the homes were similar in style and size. "I can already see this is going to be a waste of time."

"How many more do you have to check out?" Carlita asked.

"There's only one more. Remember Tony already checked out the fourth one on Baybridge Lane and the place doesn't even exist."

"That's right."

The GPS directed them to an area of downtown Savannah that was very familiar...to the spot they had followed Ben Cutler.

Chapter 13

"I knew it." Mercedes slapped her hand on the dashboard. "I thought the address looked familiar."

"I can't believe it," Carlita said as she leaned forward. "Did you ever look this place up on the internet?"

"I tried," Mercedes said. "I couldn't find anything. I couldn't even find an owner's name. It's in a trust. I tried to research the trust but ran into a dead end."

"I'm going to check it out." Carlita reached for the door handle.

Mercedes stopped her. "No. We need a plan. For all we know, there's a ring of scammers operating from this location. We can't just storm inside. Ben Cutler would recognize both of us."

"Elvira would do it." Carlita immediately dismissed the idea. Visions of Elvira charging into the building and raising a ruckus filled her head. Not only that, she was certain Elvira, aka EC Investigative Services, would charge Carlita a small fortune for her assistance. "Forget I ever mentioned her."

"Annie?" Mercedes asked.

"Nope. Ben Cutler met with her to look for an apartment."

"I've got it." Mercedes snapped her fingers. "Autumn would be perfect."

"You're right," Carlita agreed. "This would be right up her alley. The only problem is we might be putting her in harm's way."

"True." Mercedes frowned. "I would feel terrible if something happened to her."

They sat silently inside the vehicle staring at the building. A man wearing a dark jacket, the collar turned up, approached the front entrance, pulled something from his jacket pocket and then pushed the door open before stepping inside.

"I could disguise myself and go with Autumn to scope it out," Mercedes said.

On the one hand, Carlita wanted to let it go. She hoped Detective Polivich would wrap up his investigation and they wouldn't have any more incidents. Now that they had filed a police report, perhaps the ring of thieves would move on to their next target.

Still, they had lost good money and Carlita blamed herself. She left Tony with the burden of not only purchasing inventory and keeping records; he was also responsible for running the store.

Her son spent most of his waking hours working at Savannah Swag. "Let's wait until Detective Polivich finishes his investigation and then decide if we want to move forward with our own investigation."

"Okay." Mercedes sounded disappointed. Carlita reached over and patted her daughter's hand. "Don't worry. Even if this sleuthing adventure doesn't pan out, I'm sure there's another one right around the corner."

Carlita was more than a little relieved when she pulled into the parking lot and turned the car off. It took several trips for mother and daughter to unload the groceries and carry them up the stairs.

Carlita had gone slightly overboard on her spending spree, deciding more was better. There was no way she wanted to drive back to the large grocery store, at least not any time in the near future.

It took some rearranging to squeeze all of the groceries into the fridge and pantry. Her plan was to have all of the food prepped and ready for assembly early Sunday.

Mercedes helped her mother unpack and then headed downstairs to finish working on the last of the inventory. She came back to the apartment hours later, holding another bag.

Carlita, who was sitting at her desk, turned as her daughter stepped inside. "What's that?"

"More merchandise with either incorrect codes or none at all." She dropped the bag on the edge of the desk and Carlita peered inside.

"The good news is this is the last of it...I hope," Mercedes said. "Tony swears up and down he wasn't that careless with inventory."

She pulled a sapphire bracelet and signet ring from the bag and handed them to her mother. "Both of these have tags but the numbers are wrong."

Carlita turned the bracelet over and squinted her eyes at the almost illegible letters on the small tag. "How can you even read this?"

"That's part of the problem," Mercedes said. "On some of them, I can't."

Carlita studied the ring next. The handwritten letters and numbers were neatly printed on the tag. "This one is legible."

"Yeah. I found this one in the books but it doesn't match up. I'll have to sort through them to try to figure it out. I found a few that were off by either one letter or number."

Carlita carefully placed the items inside the bag. "I'm sorry Mercedes."

"It's okay. We shouldn't have any more issues now that I've got a handle on it and am taking over tracking inventory."

She thanked her daughter a second time before Mercedes told her mother she wanted to work on her book sequel, but not before mentioning she'd contacted the nearby bookstore and the owner had told her there was a group of local authors who met at the bookstore every first Thursday of the month and invited her to join them.

Carlita finished checking her email and headed downstairs to give her son a much-needed break.

Tony seemed relieved when Carlita explained why she was there. "Thanks Ma. Shelby is at work. I'm going to run down to the post office. I want to surprise her with some flowers."

Carlita grinned as she watched her son saunter out of the store. Tony, a confirmed bachelor, was in love and Carlita couldn't have been more pleased with his choice than if she'd chosen Shelby herself.

Melody, the new part-time employee Tony was training, was on hand to help. She didn't seem quite as standoffish as she had the other day and was more than willing to jump in and assist customers.

The afternoon flew by as customers came and went. Several individuals stopped in, hoping to pawn merchandise and Carlita reluctantly told them the person who purchased inventory would not be back until the following morning.

It was a shame she had to turn them away because several of the items looked like stuff they could easily sell but Carlita was wary of purchasing anything and vowed to have Tony teach her what to look for and what to offer.

The crowds thinned and Melody left for the day after finishing her shift. It was late afternoon and Carlita sat staring out the window, watching pedestrians pass by. She slid off the stool to stretch. Her leg had gone numb from sitting too long.

She limped toward the front of the store and watched as a familiar figure wandered by. It was a tall man, thin and with dark hair. When he peered inside the window, their eyes met. It was Ben Cutler.

Carlita's momentary shock was quickly replaced by anger. The man was stalking her...stalking them! She flung the front door open and darted onto the sidewalk.

Ben Cutler rounded the corner and disappeared from sight.

Carlita started to chase after him, to demand to know why he was stalking them but remembered she was the only one running the store.

"That does it. I'm going to find out what the man's problem is if it's the last thing I do." She stomped inside the store and slammed the door shut.

Carlita was still fuming when Mercedes wandered in to check on her mother. "Everything okay? You look like you're ready to spit bullets."

"I watched Ben Cutler walk by here not ten minutes ago," Carlita said. "It's obvious he's spying on us."

"Maybe he was just in the neighborhood and passing by," Mercedes theorized.

"Passing by? We're on the edge of downtown. It's not like we're in the riverfront district or the City Market. No. He's spying on us and it's time to find out why."

Adele showed up moments later. "Sorry I'm late. I had to pick up some prescriptions at the drugstore for my grandfather and they were slow."

"It's okay Adele," Carlita said. "Is your grandfather ill?"

"He was sick. He still has a nasty cough but at least he's eating now." Adele slipped her purse behind the counter. "I don't think I'll be able to make it to your party Sunday night but thank you for inviting me."

"You're welcome. I hope he's gets better soon." Carlita waited for the young woman to settle in before Mercedes and she headed out and up the stairs. "Would you like me to see if

181

Autumn has time to stop by so we can plot out a plan to turn the tables on Cutler and spy on him?"

The man was making Carlita nervous. It was as if they were part of a cat and mouse game. He didn't seem the least concerned they knew he was stalking them. In fact, it was almost as if he wanted them to know he was around.

Carlita had a choice. She could stand by and wait for him to show his hand or play defense and try to figure out "who" Ben Cutler was and what he was up to. "I'm not 100% on board with sending you two in to scope out that building and its occupants but I don't know what else to do, other than confront him and tell him I know he doesn't work for the IRS and that he lied to me."

"Lying isn't a crime," Mercedes pointed out.

"True." Carlita sighed heavily. "Yeah. Give Autumn a call and ask her if she would be willing to help us out...again."

"If we come up with a plan to get into the building I'll need a disguise," Mercedes said.

"Yes, you will." She studied her daughter's long dark locks and petite frame.

"I've always wanted to find out what it was like to be blonde," Mercedes joked. "Too bad we don't sell wigs in our store."

Carlita tilted her head. "We don't have wigs or disguises, but I know someone who might."

Chapter 14

"As a matter of fact, I have some disguises on hand." Elvira waved Mercedes and her mother into her apartment. "I'll have to charge you a small rental fee, depending on what you decide to use. Not because I'm el cheapo. You know that's not the case. It's just that I'm making payments on the stuff."

She led them to the spare bedroom and flipped the light on. Lining the entire wall were foam mannequin heads. Atop each head was a different hairpiece. There were long ones, short ones, blonde, black, curly and straight. Some of the faces sported moustaches while others displayed thick bushy eyebrows.

"Oh my gosh!" Carlita's hand flew to her mouth. "This is..."

"Pretty cool, huh?" Elvira beamed with pride. "I've got a small fortune right here in this room. I even added my collection to my renter's insurance. Never know when this place is going to burn to the ground and take all my worldly possessions with it."

"Bite your tongue," Carlita said.

Elvira ignored the comment as she reached out and flipped the tips of a blonde wig. She tapped the tip of her finger on her chin as she studied Mercedes. "So you wanna be a blonde?"

"Red is nice." Elvira pointed at a curly red wig. "This one right here is the first one I tried out a couple weeks ago when a man hired me to spy on his lover. Caught him and his secret rendezvous out at Privy Bay. The two of them were going at it hot and heavy in the backseat..."

Carlita cut her off. "Let's just leave the rest to our imagination." She turned to her daughter. "This is your operation. I'll let you pick out your disguise."

Mercedes slowly studied the different disguises. Elvira followed Mercedes around the room. "You sure you don't need my help? Granted, you and your friend have had some luck solving recent mysteries but this might be something to leave to the professionals."

"What professional?" Carlita couldn't help herself.

Elvira shot her a dark look.

Mercedes ran the palm of her hand over the top of a curly blonde wig and then kept moving. "Three of us might look suspicious. We're going to go in pretending to be looking for an address down the street and we got lost."

"Ah." Elvira nodded. "What are you going to tell them you're looking for?"

"A downtown location that placed an ad for retail space. We're interested in opening a photography studio."

"Clever," Elvira said.

"The goal is to get our foot in the door and take a look around. I tried searching the internet several times and nothing is coming up on this place. It's almost as if it doesn't exist."

"I'm going to drive the getaway car and wait for them out front while they check it out," Carlita said.

"This one will work." Mercedes carefully removed a platinum blonde wig.

"Let's give 'er a test run." Elvira reached inside a small bin near the door and pulled out a container filled with ponytail holders and bobby pins. "You'll have to put your hair up."

Mercedes deftly smoothed her hair in a ponytail, twirled it around a few times and pinned her long locks. She stepped over to a large oval mirror hanging on the wall and gently eased the wig into place.

Carlita stood behind her daughter and gazed at her reflection in the mirror. "My goodness.

The wig makes you look so different. I almost didn't recognize you."

"The eyebrows are a little dark for the hair color but that's not uncommon," Elvira said. "Most blondes are fake anyway."

Mercedes turned her head to the right and then the left as she studied her reflection. "This is perfect."

"How much to borrow...rent the wig?" Carlita asked.

Elvira pursed her lips thoughtfully. "Well. You're my first rental and I'm not sure what the market is getting for disguises." She shifted her gaze. "Forty-five dollars for twenty-four hours?"

"Forty-five dollars?' Carlita gasped. "I'm almost positive I could *buy* a new wig for that kind of money."

"Twenty-five?" Elvira asked hopefully.

"I'll give you ten bucks for two days. Forty-eight hours," Carlita said.

"It's a deal," Elvira said. "Can you pay up front?"

"Good heavens." Carlita rolled her eyes. "I'll be right back." She marched out of the apartment and across the hall. She pulled two fives from her wallet, folded them in half and returned to Elvira's spare bedroom where she held out the money.

Elvira counted the money and shoved it in her shirt pocket. "You sure you don't need anything else? Trenchcoat? Dark sunglasses? Briefcase?"

"The wig is all I need," Mercedes removed the hairpiece and pulled out the ponytail holder. She ran her fingers through her hair to fluff it out.

Elvira walked them to the door. "Be careful with the wig. If you return the merchandise and it's damaged, you'll have to pay for a replacement."

Mercedes snorted. "I'll be extra careful," she promised.

Mother and daughter stepped into the hall and Elvira closed the door behind them. "I still need to get a key for her unit since she changed the locks. Which reminds me, we need to change the lock on our door." Carlita lowered her voice. "It's not that I don't trust Elvira but I don't trust her."

Elvira was kind enough to loan them a foam mannequin head and Mercedes took that and the wig to her room while Carlita retrieved the lockset.

She had splurged and purchased a more expensive electronic door lock, which would come in handy if they ever lost their house key. It took mother and daughter less than an hour to install the electronic lock. They were able to use the existing holes so they didn't have to dig out the power tools.

Carlita was proud they were able to tackle the project on their own and didn't have to bother Tony. They also installed a single cylinder deadbolt above the electronic lock to use when they were home alone at night.

Autumn arrived as they were wrapping up the project and the trio gathered at the dining room table to discuss the plan. It was simple and, in a nutshell, exactly what they'd told Elvira.

The girls would visit the E.L. Ivey building on Bay Street, claiming to be lost and looking for an address farther down.

"Hopefully there's at least a lobby or foyer," Mercedes said.

"I tried to do some research on the building earlier while I was at work but there wasn't much to go on," Autumn said. "The E.L. Ivey building was built by Edward Louis Ivey, a local attorney, back in the 1890's. Mr. Ivey represented many of the Savannah business owners in the cotton manufacturing business."

"So it's a business," Carlita chimed in.

"Well. Maybe," Autumn said. "Over the years it's been used for both commercial and residential purposes. About ten years ago, there was a fire on the second floor and the building suffered severe smoke damage. Someone by the name of Pfinster purchased the damaged building and renovated it."

"Renovated it?"

"Yeah," Autumn nodded. "That's the weird part. No one seems to know what's inside."

"It's in a trust now. I don't think they're apartments," Mercedes said. "I was all over the internet and am pretty certain the building doesn't house tenants."

"It's a mystery." Autumn glanced at her watch. "I promised to head over to the tattoo shop. Steve and I are going to Blue Beam. It's a new restaurant off Oglethorpe Avenue. You want to come?"

"I'll pass," Carlita said. "You should go Mercedes."

"I've been meaning to run by the Book Nook to check it out. Maybe I can do it in the morning instead," Mercedes said. "Are you sure you don't mind a third wheel tagging along?"

"You're not a third wheel," Autumn said. "I hope you like Indian food."

"I've never had Indian food."

Carlita followed the women to the door and held it open for them. "Have fun." She followed them down the steps and they parted ways when the girls headed to the alley and Carlita headed inside the store.

She was on the fence about telling her son the girls were going to scope out the Ivey building. She finally decided he had enough to worry about so she didn't bring it up.

Carlita and her son spent the rest of the workday rearranging several of the display racks so there was better traffic flow. After finishing the project, she straightened several shelves and then cleaned the store's restroom.

The store was busy for a Thursday evening and Carlita was thankful for the business. The first few weeks they were open, the pawnshop had operated in the red, losing money every day. A week ago, they began breaking even and she hoped soon that they would be turning a profit.

"Where's Adele?" Carlita climbed on the barstool as Tony made his way to the back.

"I sent her home. She said she was worried about her grandfather and wanted to get his prescription to him before he went to bed."

"Have you given anymore thought to who you want to offer more hours to?" Carlita had decided to let Tony make the decision.

"Josh. I like Adele and Melody. Adele is a hard worker but with her grandfather ill and everything, I don't think she wants more hours. Melody hasn't worked here long enough for me to make a call. Plus, sometimes she cops an attitude."

"What kind of attitude?"

"The cocky kind."

"I see," Carlita said. "We're making a small profit now so I think it would be safe to ask Josh."

"Yeah," Tony nodded. "Josh is working tomorrow. I'll talk to him about it when he gets here." He slumped into the office chair and leaned back. "I found a box of baseball cards in the collector's case with the wrong tag."

"I thought Mercedes finished inventorying and caught everything," Carlita said.

"She musta missed one. The handwriting on the tag is mine," Tony said. "I checked it against Mercedes' new spreadsheet and the tag on the cards belonged on a drone."

"A drone?"

"You know, one of those remote control helicopters that glide in the air while recording video."

"Right." Carlita thought of Tinker, Annie's robot.

"I put the tag back on the drone box and labeled the baseball cards but couldn't find a record of them." Tony shrugged. "Maybe I'm losing my mind and you should fire me."

Despite the seriousness of the situation, Carlita smiled. "Oh no. You're not getting away that easy. We'll figure it out. How many items do we have for sale?"

"Thousands. A lot."

"It would be easy to make a mistake, especially when we first opened and you took on the brunt of inventorying all those items in a short amount of time," Carlita said. "Don't be so hard on yourself."

She glanced at the clock on the wall. "It's closing time. Mercedes is having dinner with Autumn and Steve. Why don't we have dinner, just the two of us?"

Tony grinned. "Sounds good. It's either eat with you or nuke a fried chicken frozen dinner in the microwave." He headed to the front, locked the entrance door and turned the sign.

"How's the apartment working out?" The last time she'd been inside her son's studio apartment was right after Bob Lowman finished remodeling it.

While Tony had flown back to Queens to pack his belongings and tie up some loose ends before returning to Savannah for good, Carlita had worked with Bob to transform the unused space in the back of the pawnshop into a sleek, modern efficiency apartment.

Bob had done a fine job of making the most of the limited space. The apartment appeared larger than it actually was and even succeeded in giving it a loft feel by tearing out the drop ceiling to expose the ductwork and pipes.

The kitchen area, though small, had everything needed to whip up a gourmet dinner.

He'd even installed a built-in convection oven and a wine fridge.

The kitchen opened to a small eat-in dining area. The living room/bedroom combo was spacious and Tony had opted to install a Murphy bed versus a regular bed to save space.

The bathroom was modern and masculine with a seamless glass shower and it sported gray and black glass tiles. Next to the shower was a vessel sink vanity with storage cabinets underneath. The only windows to the outside world were a large picture window in the living area and a small frosted window in the shower.

Tony assured his mother it didn't bother him since he didn't spend a lot of time inside.

Her son shut off the store lights, locked the door and they wandered into the alley. "What sounds good for dinner? My treat," Carlita said.

"I've been craving Mexican food, a nice big beef burrito with loads of melted cheese on top."

"There's a little hole in the wall a couple blocks from here," Carlita said. "I've never been there but sometimes those dives have the best food."

The evening air was warm and a southerly breeze rustled the leaves on the nearby oak trees lining the street.

Carlita linked arms with her son as they walked.

"I was thinking about asking Shelby if she wanted to drive up to Charleston for the day. They got some kind of art show down by the water. Art in the park or somethin'. She keeps talkin' about it."

"When is it?" Carlita asked.

"At the end of the month. It runs for a couple weeks but I was thinkin' maybe a Sunday trip since she works during the week and some Saturdays," Tony said. "Shelby would need a babysitter. I don't think Violet would appreciate viewing art," her son hinted.

"I didn't know *you* appreciated art," Carlita teased. "Of course I would love to watch Violet. We'll have fun."

"Thanks Ma."

"Speaking of art, did you know Elvira is an artist?"

Tony snorted. "She dabbles in everything."

Carlita thought of the array of disguises in Elvira's spare bedroom. "You have no idea."

The small restaurant was busy but the hostess was able to find a quiet table for two near the front. Tony ordered their specialty, a beef burrito with a side of rice and beans, while Carlita ordered the chicken fajitas.

The sizzling plate of fajitas arrived a short time later. The server slid the plate in front of Carlita and the savory smell of the grilled chicken caused her stomach to grumble.

Tony eyed her plate. "Those look good."

"So does your beef burrito," Carlita said as the server eased a plate in front of Tony.

"We'll see." Tony sawed off one end of the burrito and a huge glob of melted cheddar cheese clung to the plate and his fork. He chewed for several seconds and then nodded. "Okay, mine's better."

Carlita spread a spoonful of sour cream and salsa on top of the grilled onions and green peppers, folded the sides of the tortilla and took a big bite. There was just a hint of heat to the salsa and meat. Mixed with the sour cream, it was perfect. "I don't think so."

It was a relaxing dinner and Carlita enjoyed the evening alone with her middle son. They were so busy worrying about and running the business, there was little time for anything else.

Although they did a little "shop talk" they also discussed Tony's older brother, Vinnie, and his younger brother, Paulie, who lived in Clifton

Falls, New York with his wife, Gina and their triplets Gracie, Noel and Paulie, Jr.

The dinner portions were huge and both of them ended up with to-go boxes. Tony waited out on the sidewalk while Carlita paid.

"Before I forget, Shelby said she and Violet will stop by for the second half of the party Sunday," Tony said as he grabbed the leftovers. "She's got Sunday off but can't stay out too late since she has to work Monday morning."

"Perfect. I'm sure the party will wind down early so they can settle in for the night and our guests won't disturb them." They strolled back to the apartment and when they got there, Carlita insisted Tony keep the leftovers before they parted ways in the hall. "Why don't you let me open up in the morning? It'll be good for me to learn the routine so I know what's going on."

Tony started to argue but eventually caved and told his mother he would see her sometime the next morning and that he might actually sleep in for a change.

Mercedes was already home when Carlita got there. She'd left a note on the kitchen counter, telling her mother she had a headache and had gone to bed early but not to worry about walking Rambo. She'd already taken him out.

It had been a long day and Carlita decided to turn in early as well since she would have to be up early the next morning to open the pawnshop.

For the first time in a long time, Carlita slept through the night. Perhaps it was installing the new locks and knowing no one, including Elvira, would be sneaking inside. Perhaps it was the relaxing evening spent with her son or maybe she was exhausted. Whatever the reason, Carlita woke early the next morning full of energy and ready to start the day.

She made it to the store with a couple minutes to spare. Carlita had no more turned the sign to *Open* when her first customer entered the store...or at least she thought it was her first customer. It was Detective Polivich.

Chapter 15

Carlita said the first thing that popped into her head. "I hope you have some good news."

"I have good and bad news," the detective said. "Which would you like to hear first?"

"The good news."

"Lyla Crenshaw, the woman who claims you were trying to sell her stolen jewelry is MIA. We've left several messages on her cell phone and attempted to track her down at her job and her home. It's as if she dropped off the face of the earth. Without a complainant, we have no case."

"Which means we're free to sell the merchandise she claimed was hers?" Carlita asked.

"Yes. You may want to wait a few more days but technically, if we have no complainant, we have nothing to investigate."

"I see. That is good news. What about the purported sellers of the merchandise?"

"One of the sellers gave you a bogus address." The detective fished inside his front pocket, pulled out a notepad and flipped it open. "Dawson Greene. 272 E. Baybridge Lane. The location does not exist."

"My..." Carlita was about to say her son already checked it out but didn't want him to think they were interfering in a police investigation. "We suspected this might be the case. What about the other one?"

Mercedes and she had done a drive by of the other seller's home. Nothing looked unusual or odd.

"We talked to the property owner and he claims he never sold merchandise to Savannah Swag."

"So it's a good thing this Lyla Crenshaw has disappeared, at least for us it is."

"Correct. It's showing all the signs of a scam. There's no way to stop criminals from coming in here, using fake ID's and selling you stolen merchandise. Unfortunately, that's part of the bad news."

"Which is?"

"We've had a string of home robberies in the Garrett district." Detective Polivich flipped the page of his notepad. "I have some specific items and hope you don't mind if I take a look around."

"Not at all," Carlita said. "We have nothing to hide."

The detective wandered around the store with his notepad in hand. When he reached the area displaying the electronic devices and equipment, he stopped.

Carlita's heart plummeted as he stared at his open notepad and then the shelf. Finally, he reached over, picked up a box and studied it for a long time.

He brought it over to where Carlita was standing and placed it on the counter. "Do you mind if I open this up and take a look inside?"

"Of course not. What is it?"

"It's a drone." Detective Polivich flipped open the lid, pulled out the device and turned it over in his hand before reaching inside his pocket and slipping his glasses on. "The product codes on the bottom of these are so small you need a microscope just to read them."

"I can help," Carlita offered. "What am I reading?"

"This set of numbers." He pointed to the bottom of the device.

Carlita read the set of numbers after putting her own reading glasses on while the detective studied his notepad. When she finished, she looked up. "Let me guess. This item was reported stolen."

"Unfortunately, it was. There were several other items reported stolen as well but I don't see them in here...just this." He placed the item back inside the box and closed the lid.

"If it makes you feel any better, the other pawnshop in town, Paradise Pawn, has had similar incidents of stolen merchandise showing up in their store. We're noticing an uptick in the number of burglaries these past couple of weeks and have started a full investigation."

"Do you think the scammers and the robberies are related?"

"It could be," the detective said. "Still, we're not ruling anything out. I know you're new to this business. Are you fingerprinting the sellers?"

"I-I don't know." Carlita wasn't certain. Tony had never mentioned fingerprinting and she'd never seen him fingerprint anyone.

"If you're not then I suggest you start, at least until we apprehend the person or persons who are breaking into area homes and stealing property."

"I appreciate the suggestion," Carlita said.

The detective picked up the box and tucked it under his arm. "I need to take this with me as evidence." He patted the top.

"Of course." Carlita followed the detective to the front door. "Wait. I have a suspicious person who filled out an application to rent one of my vacant apartments. I found out he gave me false information." She went on to tell the detective the man returned with a box full of merchandise to pawn. Carlita left out the part about following him.

"I saw him walk by our store yesterday," Carlita said. Even as the words came out of her mouth, she knew she sounded silly. So the man lied and then came back to sell some unwanted items. Neither of those was a crime.

"I guess it was nothing," she trailed off.

The detective left, promising to call her when he had news and Josh showed up to start his shift so Carlita headed upstairs. Mercedes was already up and dressed. "Autumn is on her way over. We were thinking of heading over to Bay Street this morning."

Carlita thought of the detective, the string of robberies and the stolen merchandise which kept showing up in her store. "That's fine with me. The sooner the better."

***

Carlita slowed the car and stared at the only empty parallel parking spot. The last time Mercedes and she had visited Bay Street, the spots had been wide open and it had been easy for her to drive into the open spot and then pull right back out.

This time, there were cars in the way...a whole row of cars. "I don't think I can do this. This car is a tank and the empty parking spot is too small."

Mercedes eyed the spot. "You have plenty of room. This will be a good lesson on parallel parking." She turned to her friend. "Tell her how to do it Autumn."

"Me?" Autumn squeaked. "I think the only time I paralleled parked was during driver's ed."

"I've never tried it before," Mercedes admitted.

Carlita stopped in the middle of the road and a car horn honked behind them.

"Put your turn signal on so they know we're taking the spot," Mercedes said.

Carlita turned her signal on, rolled the window down and motioned the impatient driver to go around.

She waited until the car sped past. "Now what?"

"Pull ahead so you're parallel with the car in front, shift into reverse and then lightly crank the wheel as you steer into the spot," Autumn instructed.

"Easier said than done," Carlita muttered as she shifted the car into reverse. She pressed the gas a little too hard. The tires spun.

Mercedes squeezed her eyes shut and braced for the coming jolt, which was more like a light tap.

Autumn, who was sitting in the back seat, peered out the back window. "You nailed the parking meter."

"Oh my gosh." Carlita panicked, shifted into drive and pressed the gas. She pulled into oncoming traffic and the path of a car that was maneuvering around their parking attempt.

Carlita came within inches of hitting the vehicle as she stomped on the brakes. "I-I can't do this."

"You have to," Mercedes said. "It's the only open spot, unless you want to drop us off and park somewhere else. I can call you when we're done."

There was no way Carlita could do that. She wanted to be able to keep an eye on the building...and the girls, in case they ran into a problem. She needed to be in that spot. "No way. I'll try again."

She pulled next to the car in front again, took a deep breath, shifted into reverse and then gently applied a small amount of pressure to the gas pedal as she steered the car and checked her passenger side mirror.

"You're doing good," Autumn reported. "Keep going...going. Crank the wheel a little more to the right and...you've got it."

"Now straighten the wheel and pull ahead a little," Mercedes said.

Carlita did as her daughter told her. "I did it! I wonder if I dinged the bumper when I hit the meter."

"I'll check it out." Autumn flung the back door open and hopped onto the curb. She hurried to the back of the car to inspect the bumper. After a quick inspection, she jogged to the passenger side window. "There's a small scratch on the passenger side corner but nothing that can't be buffed out."

"Mercedes did that a couple months ago when she had a run in with the dumpster," Carlita said as she shut the car off. "We need to feed the parking meter." She eased out of the car and made her way to the meter. After reading the instructions, she inserted her credit card and paid for an hour of parking before slipping back behind the wheel.

Mercedes lowered the passenger side visor and peered into the mirror as she smoothed several loose strands of the blonde wig. She gazed at her friend, standing on the curb. "Are you ready to get this mission under way?"

Autumn grinned and patted her front pocket. "You bet. Let's get this show on the road."

Chapter 16

Mercedes strode toward the nondescript double doors of the E.L. Ivey building. She gave her mother, who was watching them through the front windshield, a quick look and grabbed the door handle.

Autumn, who was standing next to her, gave her a gentle nudge. "This is going to be a piece of cake."

"I hope you're right." A sudden feeling of foreboding filled Mercedes as she opened the door and the women stepped into the small lobby. Lining both walls were rows of mailboxes. On the far wall were two elevators.

"This is it?" Autumn wrinkled her nose as she looked around.

There's a directory on the wall." Mercedes pointed toward the elevators and a black display board.

They stepped over to the board and studied the list. "Bruin and Stein Law Offices, Killian Dental Group, Georgia Insurance Group." Mercedes rattled off the list of businesses. "This definitely isn't a residential building." She finished scanning the list and when she got to the last one, she paused. There was no name, only initials. "I wonder what the SGCPO is."

"There's only one way to find out." Autumn stepped in front of the elevator on the right and pressed the *up* button. Nothing happened so she pressed it a second time.

"Let me try." Mercedes slipped past her friend and jabbed the *up* button with her thumb. "Maybe it's out of service. Let's see if the other elevator works." She started toward the second elevator and Autumn held up a hand. "You need a special access card to use it." She pointed to a thin slot on the front panel, next to the doors.

"Great. I hope they're both not keycard-only elevators." Mercedes pressed the other up button. The elevator made a faint whooshing noise before the doors silently opened.

The women stepped inside and Mercedes stared at the display of buttons. "What floor was the "S" whatever on?"

"I forgot." Autumn hurried from the elevator while Mercedes held the doors open. She quickly scanned the display and then hopped back inside the elevator. "It's on the twelfth floor."

Mercedes studied the rows of buttons. "There is no twelfth floor. It only goes to eleven." She was even more curious to find out what was on the twelfth floor. "I have an idea." She pushed the "11" button and the elevators doors slid shut.

When the elevator reached the eleventh floor, the doors opened and they stepped out into a small hall. There was a door to the left and a door to the right. They stepped to the door on the left. "Savannah Food Group."

Mercedes shifted her gaze to the other door. "Streamline Beverage Company."

"I guess you know what floor to hop off on if you're hungry or thirsty," Autumn joked.

Mercedes reached for the Savannah Food Group door handle.

"What are you doing?"

"I'm going in," Mercedes said as she twisted the knob and opened the door.

The interior was a large, lofty space. On one side were several chairs and a coffee table. On the other was an L-shaped receptionist desk. The woman sitting behind the desk eyed them curiously. "Can I help you?"

"Yes. I mean, I hope so," Mercedes said. "We were across the hall, meeting with someone from the beverage company and were getting ready to leave. I needed to use their restroom and they said it was temporarily out of order and suggested I come over here to use your facilities."

The woman raised a brow. "Oh really?" She cleared her throat. "I guess it would be okay." She shifted in her chair and pointed down a narrow hall, between two rows of dark brown cubicles. "Go to the end of this hall and take a left. The restroom is in the back. There's only one stall. You'll have to take turns."

"Thanks so much." Mercedes smiled as she tugged on Autumn's arm and they hurried in the direction the woman pointed. When they got to the end, Mercedes stopped.

"The restroom is over there," Autumn said.

"I don't have to go to the bathroom," Mercedes whispered. "I'm looking for the stairwell or fire escape."

"I see it," Autumn whispered.

"Where?"

"Over there. It's the door marked *stairs*."

"Duh." With a quick glance behind her, Mercedes darted to the door. Autumn was hot on her heels.

Mercedes twisted the knob, eased the creaky door open and slipped inside.

Autumn followed her into the stairwell and Mercedes eased the squeaky door shut before shifting her attention to the rusty metal railing and dull gray concrete steps.

Autumn shivered as she eyed the stairwell. "I'm positive I saw these stairs in the movie *Stalker in the Stairwell*."

"I believe it." Mercedes looked up. "Let's go." She hurried to the steps and began climbing.

"I dunno about this." Autumn reluctantly followed her friend up the steps.

The stairwell ended abruptly in front of a black metal door.

"This has to be it." Mercedes twisted the knob. "The door is locked."

"Let me try." Autumn grabbed the knob. "Yep. We reached another dead end...literally."

"Can you pick the lock?" Mercedes asked.

"I didn't bring my tool. I didn't know I was going to have to pick locks. All I have is my stun gun and cell phone."

"So close and yet so far." Mercedes studied the door before pressing her ear against it. "I can't hear anything." She lifted her head, clenched her fists and began to pound on the door. "Hello!" she yelled.

"What are you doing?" Autumn hissed.

The door abruptly flew open and a man wearing thick black glasses and a scowl on his face stood on the other side.

"I...we were on a lower level, trying to find the restrooms but ended up in the stairwell. When we tried to get back inside, the door was locked," Mercedes fibbed. "I was wondering if we could use your restroom and also the elevator."

The man started to close the door in her face.

Mercedes shoved her foot in the frame. "You're not going to just leave us out here."

"This floor is off limits to the public."

"If you don't let me in, I'm going to leave a big wet puddle right here." Mercedes pointed at the floor in front of the door.

"So?" the man grunted but Mercedes stared him down, refusing to remove her foot.

"All right but hurry up. The bathroom is over here." He led them through a maze of cubicles, similar to the ones on the floor below, to a corner and a door with a large "W" on the front. "Do what you have to do." He stood guard and stared at them pointedly.

Mercedes hurried into the small bathroom. Inside was a single sink, a toilet and a shower stall. She eased the flimsy blue shower curtain to the left. It was empty except for a bottle of shampoo and bar of soap.

She quietly slid the curtain shut and began rifling through the small cabinet under the sink. Inside were rolls of paper towels, toilet paper and a bottle of liquid hand soap. Tucked in the corner was a small cardboard box.

Mercedes shot a quick glance at the bathroom door, flushed the toilet and turned the faucets on full blast before reaching inside the cabinet and pulling out the box. On the front of the box was a shipping label. "Bingo." She tilted it toward the light. *SGCPO, 119 Bay Street, Savannah, Georgia.* It was another dead end.

Mercedes turned the water off and carefully placed the box under the cabinet before closing the doors and exiting the restroom.

The frowning man and Autumn stood waiting on the other side. "Your turn."

"I don't…" Autumn was about to say "have to go," but the look on Mercedes face told her she *did* need to go. "I'll be right back." She hurried into the restroom and closed the door behind her.

Mercedes turned her attention to the man. "So what kind of business is this? Let me guess – it's the corporate office for a security company."

The man's scowl deepened.

"A top secret government lab?"

"Your friend better hurry up," he replied.

Autumn emerged from the bathroom a few minutes later. "Thank you for allowing us to use the facilities."

The man cleared his throat. "I'll escort you out." He didn't wait for an answer as he turned on his heel and began marching down the center hall.

Mercedes hung back in an attempt to catch a glimpse of what was behind the tall gray dividers. Several were empty while others were occupied. She could hear the low murmur of voices but wasn't able to catch a single word being said.

They passed by a reception area, similar to the one on the floor below.

The man opened the hall door and waited for Mercedes and Autumn to join him before leading the way to a single elevator. He pressed the down arrow.

Mercedes decided to give it one final shot. "I'm sorry. I didn't catch your name."

He glared at her silently.

The doors open and he motioned them inside.

"Thanks so much for your hospitality," Mercedes said sarcastically. The doors started to close. "It was nice talking to you!"

The doors closed and the elevator began its descent. "What was that all about?" Autumn asked.

"I have no idea but I want to take a picture of the display when we reach the lobby. Maybe we can figure out what SGCPO stands for."

The doors opened and the girls stepped out onto the ground floor lobby and almost ran smack dab into Ben Cutler, who was waiting for the elevator they were exiting.

Chapter 17

Mercedes lowered her head as she hurried past Cutler.

Autumn hung back and watched as Cutler pulled a keycard from his pocket and slid it into the slot. The elevator doors opened and he stepped inside. The doors closed and she turned to Mercedes. "I thought you wanted a picture of the listing."

"I almost forgot." Mercedes hurried to the display, pulled her cell phone from her back pocket, switched it to camera mode and then snapped a picture. She glanced at the elevator doors. "That was Ben Cutler, the guy we've been telling you about."

"Him?' Autumn asked. "He was cute."

"He's a liar," Mercedes said bluntly. "He told us he just took a job with the IRS and they've never heard of him."

"So he fibbed. I mean, everybody fibs at least once in a while."

"He's too old for you," Mercedes said. "Well, whatever Mr. Cutler does, it involves the business on the twelfth floor."

The women exited the building and strode to the car.

Mercedes climbed into the passenger seat while Autumn slid into the back.

"I saw Ben Cutler enter the building a couple minutes ago. Did he see you? Did he recognize you?" Carlita asked.

"Nope, at least I don't think he recognized me. The E.L. Ivey building is full of offices. There's an attorney's office, a dentist office, an office for a restaurant group and a beverage company."

"There aren't any apartments?"

"Nope." Autumn shook her head. She went on to explain to Carlita how there were two elevators. "The entire twelfth floor is occupied by a company or business with the initials SGCPO."

"What is SGCPO?"

"We have no idea," Autumn said. "You could only get to the top floor using a second elevator and the only way to use the elevator is if you had a special keycard."

"So you didn't get a chance to see it?"

"Oh, we saw it all right. Mercedes was on her game. We took the elevator to the eleventh floor and then used the stairs to access the next level." Autumn told Carlita how they had managed to scope out the mysterious business but still had no idea what it was.

"I watched Ben Cutler use a keycard to access the private twelfth floor elevator," Autumn said.

"How do you know the second elevator is only for the top floor?" Carlita glanced in her side mirror, shifted into drive and eased out of the parking spot.

"Because one of the goons who works on the mysterious twelfth floor escorted us to the elevator," Mercedes said. "When we got inside, I checked out the panel. The elevator only goes to one floor...twelve."

When they got home, Mercedes and Autumn headed to Mercedes' computer to begin combing the internet while Carlita fixed several turkey on rye with Swiss cheese sandwiches. After she finished munching on hers, she left two on the counter for Mercedes and Autumn and then told them she was heading downstairs to give Tony a break.

She entered the store through the back door. Tony was talking with a customer so she set his sandwich and napkin on the desk before sliding into the office chair.

Business was brisk for a Friday afternoon and it was another half hour before Tony was able to take a break and join his mother. He eyed the sandwich. "For me?"

"Of course." Carlita hopped out of the chair. "Why don't you get out of here for a few minutes? Josh and I can hold down the fort."

"Thanks Ma." Tony picked up his sandwich and headed to the back.

"Hello Mrs. Garlucci." Josh wandered over.

"Hello Josh. Did Tony give you the party invitation?"

"Yes ma'am. I was wondering if I could bring my girlfriend, Tiffany, with me."

"Of course. I would love to meet her." The two chatted for several moments before more customers arrived and Josh went to help them.

The store got busy as customers poured in and the next hour flew by. Carlita was thrilled she was able to sell several items. Josh was ringing up sales, too, and she couldn't wait to see the end of day total.

When Tony returned, Carlita told him she needed to get started on the prep work for the dinner party. She told Josh good-bye and that she would see him later. She started to walk to the back and Tony stopped her. "You might want to go around front. There's a large couch blocking the back door."

Carlita had almost forgotten it was Friday...moving day for Cool Bones. "I forgot Charles is moving in today," she said. "Stop by later and you can be my official taste tester. I'm making some samples for Sunday's party."

Tony promised her he would before Carlita exited through the front door and circled around back. She wondered what Cool Bones thought about Elvira's painting as she walked past a large moving truck parked in the middle of the alley.

The lower hall was full of furniture and she had to duck to avoid a mover, carrying a floor lamp as he passed her on the stairs.

She passed a second mover in the upstairs hallway. The area was a beehive of activity but there was no sign of her new tenant.

Rambo met her at the door and began wagging his tail. Carlita patted his head. "You don't want to go out there right now. How 'bout the deck instead?" She led her pooch to the deck, opened the slider and Rambo trotted out.

Grayvie followed the dog to the deck and then leapt onto one of the patio chairs to watch the movers as they unloaded the back of the truck.

Carlita headed to the kitchen to start prepping for the dinner party. As she worked, she mulled over the string of stolen merchandise which kept showing up in Savannah Swag. Somehow, the merchandise was making its way onto her store shelves.

The fact that Ben Cutler had lied, he was lurking about and had paid his deposit, first and last months' rent deposit in cash sent up a red flag. Who walked around with five thousand dollars in cash in their pocket?

Perhaps if Mercedes and Autumn could figure out what business was on the top floor of the E.L. Ivey building they would have their first clue as to who Ben Cutler really was.

Detective Polivich mentioned a scheme where crooks sold stolen merchandise to unsuspecting businesses and an accomplice would swoop in and claim the fenced goods were stolen from them.

She made a mental note to pass on Detective Polivich's recommendation to Tony to start fingerprinting sellers. What if sellers refused to be fingerprinted?

If they weren't doing anything wrong or illegal, why would they care? She wouldn't care if someone wanted to fingerprint her when she sold merchandise.

The detective had also mentioned they weren't the only ones who had purchased stolen merchandise. The authorities had also found stolen merchandise at Paradise Pawn.

Carlita began chopping garlic, fresh rosemary, basil and tomatoes. Next, she started on the linguine and spaghetti noodles. It took some time since she had to make enough to feed a small army.

Autumn and Mercedes emerged from the bedroom as Carlita was sautéing the garlic in butter. "What did you find out?"

"A big fat nothing," Mercedes said.

"Zero, zip, zilch," Autumn added. "There is nothing at all on the internet listing a company with the initials SGCPO."

"We think the 'G' might stand for Georgia and maybe the 'S' for south or Savannah so it might be South Georgia/Savannah, Georgia something but we're stuck after that," Mercedes said as she eyed the frying pan. "Are you prepping for the big dinner party?"

"Yes and if you're finished, I could use some help." She put Mercedes and Autumn to work dicing tomatoes and shredding large blocks of mozzarella and parmesan cheese. With all three of them working, they quickly created several sample dishes for tasting.

She whipped up a mini lasagna and spaghetti pie as well as her signature linguine. Carlita invited Autumn to stay and try the dishes but she said she needed to run some errands before it got too late. She promised she would eat her share during Sunday's party.

As if on cue, Tony arrived while Carlita was pulling the bubbling dishes from the oven. "You're right on time." She eyed the clock on the stove. "Did you close shop early?"

"No. Adele called me earlier to ask if she could work a few hours tonight to make up for having to leave early the other day so Josh and Adele are both downstairs." Tony shrugged. "I figured it was good to let them work together."

He patted his pocket. "I got my cell phone on and gave them instructions to call if they needed anything." He changed the subject. "Did you get my message?"

Carlita placed the piping hot dish of lasagna on the glass cooktop. "What message?"

"I had someone come in and ask about buying a drone. I looked for the drone we had in stock and it's gone," Tony said. "I don't see a receipt where we sold it."

Carlita dropped the potholders on the counter. "I forgot to tell you Detective Polivich stopped by first thing this morning. It seems the drone was reported stolen a couple days ago."

Tony pounded his fist on the counter in frustration. "I can't believe it."

"Well, son, we're not alone." She told him what the detective had told her, how Paradise Pawn was also purchasing stolen merchandise and detectives found several items in their store, as well. "He thinks there's a scam. A string of thieves are breaking into area homes and selling the merchandise to area pawnshops."

"Was he sure the drone was stolen?"

"Yes." Carlita nodded. "We matched the serial number on the bottom. He said the FAA now requires drones to have serial numbers since owners have to register them in order to fly them."

She went on to tell him what Mercedes and Autumn found out when they scoped out the E.L. Ivey Building.

"Hey Bro." Mercedes, who had walked Autumn out, traipsed into the kitchen.

Tony did a double take. "Whoa! What's up with the new do?"

"Do you like it?" Mercedes ran her fingers through the blonde locks. "It's kind of growing on me."

"You look weird," he said bluntly.

Mercedes whacked her brother in the arm.

"She does not," Carlita said.

"Okay. You don't look weird. You look like a freak," he joked.

Mercedes punched him again, this time harder.

"Break it up you two," Carlita said. "Let's sample the dinner items before someone gets hurt." She set several potholders in the center of the dining room table and Tony and Mercedes placed the hot dishes on top.

After the table was set, they settled in to eat. Carlita passed out the dinner plates and silverware before placing a heaping spoonful of linguine, a wedge of spaghetti pie and a piece of lasagna on her plate.

She leaned forward and breathed in the aroma of garlic and fresh basil before sampling the linguine first. "The linguine is a little dry."

"It's delicious," Tony mumbled between bites.

The spaghetti pie was next. It was also a little dry. "Two for two," she groaned.

Her final taste test was the spicy lasagna. She was on the fence about using spicy Italian sausage but to her, it was the best of the three dishes. Besides, it was too late to change her mind. She'd already cooked all of the sausage so it would be ready to assemble.

Mercedes declared her favorite to be the spaghetti pie. Tony claimed his was the linguine, which didn't surprise Carlita. It was his favorite dish.

Hers was the lasagna. Despite making small portions, there were still plenty of leftovers. "I wonder if Josh and Adele are hungry. I can make them both to-go containers and send an extra home with you, Tony, in case you get hungry later."

Tony pushed back his chair and patted his stomach. "Soon, I'm gonna have to buy bigger clothes," he complained.

Tony and Mercedes cleared the table while Carlita fixed the to-go boxes.

Knock. Knock. Carlita closed the lid on the last container, wiped her hands on the front of her apron and hurried to the door. "I wonder who that is."

She peeked through the peephole. It was her new tenant, Cool Bones. She opened the door. "Hello Charles. Cool Bones. Welcome to Walton Square."

"Thanks Mrs. Garlucci. I just wanted to apologize if I inconvenienced you today with my moving truck and moving crew."

"Not at all. Please...call me Carlita. I'd like you to meet my children," Carlita said as she waved him inside.

Mercedes and Tony met them near the door where Carlita quickly introduced them. "Charles, this is my daughter, Mercedes, and my middle son, Tony."

Cool Bones shook hands with them both. "All my friends call me Cool Bones."

He shook Mercedes' hand last. "I'm surprised with your Italian roots you have such blonde hair."

Mercedes grabbed the front of the wig and pulled it off, revealing her jet-black hair. "I'm not." She shot her mother a quick glance. "I was...uh."

"She was just testing out the theory blondes have more fun."

"It's not true," Mercedes smiled and quickly changed the subject. "How do you like your new apartment?"

"I love it so far," Cool Bones replied. "It's quiet, much quieter than my old apartment."

"How do you like your housewarming gift?" Carlita asked referring to the portrait Elvira and she had hung above the fireplace.

Cool Bones shook his head. "That Elvira. She stopped by a little while ago and brought me a large casserole dish full of food. Something called nat..."

Mercedes made a gagging noise.

Carlita gave her daughter a warning look. "It's natto, one of Elvira's favorite dishes. It has an unusual odor."

"It stinks," Mercedes said bluntly.

"According to Elvira, it's good for digestion," Carlita said. Cool Bones would find out soon enough if he liked natto. Maybe he would love it.

"I'm a meat and potatoes kind of guy myself. I tried a bite and it was...interesting. Maybe if I warm it up in the microwave it will taste better."

"Or make you throw up," Mercedes said.

"Mercedes," Carlita scolded.

"What? You know it's true."

Cool Bones apologized again before assuring Carlita he hadn't forgotten he and his band, the Jazz Boys, planned to set up in the courtyard around 5:30 Sunday evening and would play for an hour or so, until the party moved into the upper hall.

Carlita thanked him for offering to play before handing him one of the to-go boxes she'd filled with food. "Here. In case the natto doesn't work out."

"Thank you." Cool Bones sniffed the container appreciatively. "This smells heavenly."

After he left, Mercedes volunteered to load the dishwasher while Tony and Carlita headed downstairs with more of the leftovers. She asked her son if he'd offered more hours to Josh and he told her he had. Josh's hours would be Monday, Wednesday and Friday from one to close, Saturday nine until noon and Sunday noon to close.

They stepped into the back of the store, passing by the employee only area and walked onto the store floor.

The first thing Carlita noticed was that the cash register drawer was wide open. She looked around. The store appeared to be empty. It appeared empty until she spotted Josh, who was sprawled out on the floor next to the jewelry case, his eyes closed.

Chapter 18

Adele, whose hands and feet were bound, was lying on the floor on the other side of the cash register. Her eyes were wide open and filled with fear.

"Oh my gosh!" Carlita flung the food on the desk and ran across the room to Adele, who was closest. She dropped to the floor and began untying the piece of cloth covering her mouth.

"Ma! Get back behind the counter!" Tony ran from the room, returning moments later brandishing a gun.

Carlita let go of the piece of cloth and began dragging Adele to safety. Meanwhile, Tony crept forward holding the gun tightly in his hand, his eyes scanning the store aisles.

After dragging Adele behind the counter, Carlita slithered across the floor to Josh, whose eyes were still shut. She pressed two fingers to the side of his neck and felt the steady beat of his pulse. "Thank God."

Her eyes quickly scanned his body. There were no signs of injuries except for a small knot that was starting to form on the side of his forehead.

"It's clear." Tony raced to the back of the store and knelt next to Josh. "We need to call the cops and an ambulance."

"Of course." Carlita hurried to the desk phone. Her fingers trembled as she dialed 911. "Yes. This is Carlita Garlucci. I own Savannah Swag, 210 Mulberry Street. I think we were just robbed. At least one of our employees has been hurt."

The operator told her she was dispatching officers and an ambulance before she disconnected the line.

Tony was working on pulling off the cloth covering Adele's mouth. As soon as it was off, the young woman began screaming and babbling. Calita was able to catch "robbed" and "Josh."

Carlita helped her son finish removing Adele's bindings as the police arrived in a flurry of squad cars, wailing sirens and flashing lights.

"Freeze!"

Carlita and Tony lifted their hands.

"We're the owners," Tony said. "We just called this in. I already searched the place. Whoever robbed us and attacked our employees is long gone."

Carlita placed both hands on Adele's shoulders to calm her and forced the young woman to look at her. "Adele. Are you okay? Were you hurt?"

"N-no, but the robbers hit Josh on the head." She turned to Carlita, her eyes wide. "I saw him. I saw that man!"

Carlita didn't have time to ask who 'that man' was as more sirens filled the air and two paramedics raced in through the front door.

One of the police officers motioned toward Josh. "He's over here."

The EMTs worked on Josh for several long moments while Carlita prayed like she'd never prayed before. When she heard Josh moan, she burst into tears.

One of the EMTs stayed with Josh while the other hurried to the ambulance and returned with a stretcher. "It appears he may have suffered a concussion from a blow to his temple. We're going to take him to the hospital to have him checked out."

The men gently placed Josh on the stretcher before lifting it and carrying him out. One of them returned moments later. "Is there anyone else who needs medical attention?"

Carlita pointed at Adele. "She was also here when the store was robbed."

The EMT examined Adele. During the examination, she assured them she was shaken but not physically harmed and was more worried about Josh.

After the EMT finished checking Adele, he stopped to tell the officers they were transporting Josh to Savannah Regional Memorial Hospital.

One of the officers stepped forward and Carlita realized he looked familiar. She glanced at his badge. "Detective Jackson."

"Mrs. Garlucci. I thought this placed looked familiar." He turned to the other man. "This is Officer Sims."

Detective Jackson had been on scene to investigate human remains Carlita and her children recently found hidden inside a secret wall in their basement.

"What happened?"

All eyes turned to Adele. "I..." She took a shaky breath. "I came in to work late. Tony told me I could make up some hours I missed. It was around six. I was busy showing jewelry to a woman looking for a pair of earrings. Josh was near the gun rack and Tony was talking to someone interested in selling some junk." Adele corrected herself. "Some merchandise. When things slowed down, Tony asked if he could run upstairs for dinner. Josh and I told him we could handle running the store by ourselves."

She paused as if gathering her thoughts. "I remember seeing these two men pass by the front of the store a couple times. They kept staring in the window as if they were casing the joint. I was just about to tell Josh they made me nervous when they ran inside, waving guns at us and telling us to get down on the floor."

Adele's whole body began to tremble and Carlita put an arm around her shoulders. "It's okay. Take your time."

Adele nodded. "I guess Josh didn't hit the floor fast enough because one of them took the end of his gun and hit him hard. J-Josh crumpled to the floor. I thought they killed him," she whispered before bursting into tears.

The detective waited patiently for Carlita to comfort the young woman. She regained her composure and continued. "One of them broke the back of the jewelry case while the other one made me open the cash register. He took a bunch of money and shoved it into his pockets, and then pushed me on the floor and tied me up."

"Did you get a good look at them? Were they wearing masks?"

"Yeah." Adele turned to Carlita. "They were both wearing hoodies with a covering over their mouths but I swear I recognized one of them, his eyes. It was that guy you told me to keep an eye on and let you know if he ever came back into the store. You know, the tall, dark-haired man you pointed out the other day."

The blood drained from Carlita's face. Adele was talking about Ben Cutler!

"Do you know who she's talking about?" Detective Jackson asked.

"Yes. His name is Ben Cutler, at least he listed his name as Ben Cutler. He has some connection to the E.L. Ivey Building on Bay Street. He recently filled out a rental application for an apartment I had for rent," Carlita said.

"Can I see the application?" the detective asked.

"I can do one better. I'll give you a copy. It's upstairs on my desk." Carlita flew up the stairs and into the apartment. The folder was right where she'd left it but Ben Cutler's application was gone.

Chapter 19

"Oh my gosh. I hope we didn't accidentally toss out Cutler's application," she whispered to herself.

"What are you doing?" Mercedes voice echoed in Carlita's ear and she jumped. "Mercedes!"

"Sorry Ma. What are you doing?" Mercedes repeated the question.

"I'm looking for Ben Cutler's application."

"It's in my room. I was researching some of the other information he put on his application."

"I need to make a photocopy for the police," Carlita said.

"The police?"

"We were robbed. Adele thinks she recognized one of the robbers as Ben Cutler. I told the police he'd filled out an application to rent one of our apartments and they asked for a copy."

Mercedes jogged to her room, returning moments later waving the application. "We can make a copy downstairs."

The women hustled back to the store and Mercedes headed to the copy machine.

The officer and Detective Jackson were still talking to Tony and Adele. After Mercedes made a copy of both sides, she handed it to the detective.

"Thank you." He glanced at the front. "We may be able to finally get a break in the string of recent robberies that have sprung up in downtown Savannah."

He folded the application in thirds, tucked it in his notepad and placed both inside his pocket. "We'll run by the last known address for Mr. Cutler tonight, while the trail is still fresh." He turned to Adele. "I have your contact information. I may have more questions for you and will give you a call if needed."

Carlita accompanied Detective Jackson and Officer Sims and the trio stepped out onto the sidewalk. "Do you think it will be okay if we visit Josh, our employee, in the hospital later tonight?"

"It will be up to the hospital to decide if he can have visitors." Jackson nodded toward the store. "Your employee may have given us our first big break."

Carlita thanked the officer and detective for their quick response and made her way back inside.

Adele, who had so far maintained her composure during most of the questioning, began sobbing uncontrollably. Mercedes and Tony, who had been trying to comfort her, turned to their mother.

Carlita didn't do much better and finally offered to drive the young woman home. "I-I need the money."

"We'll pay you for the rest of the day," Carlita said. "Take tomorrow off. We'll pay you for that, too. One of us will take you home. Try to get some rest."

She continued. "Going forward, we'll make sure either Tony, Mercedes or I am working the floor with you, Josh and Melody."

"I-I'm okay to work tomorrow," Adele said. "I'm more concerned about Josh."

Since Saturday was their busiest day, it would help them out immensely if Adele worked the following day. "If you're sure," Carlita said.

Adele nodded. "Yes. I am."

"I'll take her home," Mercedes offered. She turned to her mother. "It's too late to inventory the stolen merchandise tonight."

"I agree. We can work on it tomorrow. As long as we're careful to log new sales before you're able to go through everything." Carlita gave the young woman a warm hug. "I'm so sorry this happened to you."

"I-it's okay. Like I said, I'm just worried about Josh."

Carlita walked them to the car while Tony stayed inside the store to wait on unsuspecting customers, who had no idea the store had just been robbed.

She was tempted to tell Tony to close after they left, but then the thugs would win. There was one thing Carlita had discovered about herself since her husband's death. She was a fighter. She'd fought long and hard to open the doors to the pawnshop.

She'd fought the city, fought one of the neighbors and even fought her tenant just to get to opening day. This was her business, her home and no one was going to keep Carlita Garlucci down!

A determined Carlita stepped back inside the store and watched as Tony helped the customers. It was time for another round of shooting practice. Not only was she going to practice, she was going to make sure they kept a loaded gun behind the counter and she would not be afraid to use it.

By the time Mercedes returned, it was almost closing time. Despite her resolve to fight, she was more than a little relieved when she turned the front window sign to *Closed* and flipped the deadbolt, locking the front door.

Mercedes and Tony stood in the back, waiting for Carlita to join them. "We need to check the video surveillance for the store."

"The police already did and there's no recording of the robbery." Tony led them to the back corner and pointed up at the surveillance camera. "It's been on the fritz for a couple days now. I've been meaning to check the connection."

Mercedes headed to the desk, slid into the chair and reached for the mouse. "Let's see if we have any footage at all." The three of them studied the surveillance video but what few images they had were blurry. None of it covered the robbery incident and during that part of the tape, all that showed was a gray, fuzzy screen.

"I'll try to fix it in the morning," Tony said.

"We should do it now," Mercedes urged. "The perp always returns to the scene of the crime."

"You think Ben Cutler is going to return here after robbing us and injuring one of our employees?" Carlita gasped.

"I found out something very interesting about Ben Cutler tonight. There was a small clue I was able to track down on his application," Mercedes said mysteriously. "Like I said, I always heard criminals are drawn to the scene of their crime."

Tony shrugged. "Okay. But I can do it first thing in the morning."

Mercedes was insistent her brother fix the equipment and not wait until morning.

The two bickered back and forth for several moments until Carlita stepped in. "Mercedes may be right. If for no other reason than to keep an eye on the place, we should at least try to fix it."

"Okay. I guess I'm out numbered," Tony grumbled as he headed to the storeroom to retrieve his ladder. Fortunately, it was only a loose wire. They tested the repaired surveillance equipment and it worked like a charm.

"See? That wasn't so bad," Carlita said. "We can wait to fix the broken display cabinet door in the morning.

Tony put the ladder away while Carlita double-checked the perimeter doors and windows and Mercedes moved the merchandise from the broken cabinet to another cabinet.

While Tony and Mercedes finished up, Carlita called Savannah Memorial Hospital to inquire on Josh's condition. The receptionist told her he was doing well, but had been admitted and would be staying overnight for observation.

Carlita thanked the woman and then relayed the information to her children. Josh was going to be all right. "After Adele arrives for work tomorrow, Mercedes and I can run over to the hospital to check on Josh and see if he remembers anything."

"The police will probably already have talked to him by then," Mercedes pointed out.

"But if they talk to him tonight, he might not remember everything," her mother insisted. "Plus he may be in shock."

"True," Mercedes said. "I know I'd be a wreck if I was robbed at gunpoint and knocked unconscious."

Carlita hugged her son and clung to him for a couple extra seconds. It could easily have been

Tony inside the store when it was robbed and knowing her son, he would have put up a fight. She shivered as she thought about what might have happened to him. It was horrible enough Josh was injured and Adele scared half to death.

Carlita grabbed the original copy of Ben Cutler's application on her way out of the store and waited in the hall while Tony turned off the lights and locked the door. She promised her son she would meet him at the store to open at nine.

Saturday was the busiest day of the week and with Josh in the hospital and Adele not scheduled to come in until eleven, they would need an extra set of hands on deck to run the store.

Mercedes said she would help, too, and after another quick hug, Mercedes and Carlita climbed the stairs to their apartment while Tony headed to his apartment.

Carlita waited until they were inside and the door closed and locked before she spoke. "What if Ben Cutler doesn't return to the scene of the crime?" she asked.

"I don't think the person who robbed the store was Ben Cutler," she said matter-of-factly. "It was someone else."

"Who?" Carlita asked.

"I don't want to point fingers. Let's just say I think we're going to uncover the criminals or at least one of them tomorrow."

Despite Carlita's attempts to get Mercedes to spill the beans, her daughter refused, saying she believed they would find out soon enough.

Mercedes had a plan. Now all she had to do was wait for the unsuspecting suspect to walk right into it. "I'll give you a clue Ma. Think motive and opportunity. If you can figure out who had motive and opportunity to commit the almost perfect crime, you'll be close to figuring out the whodunit."

Chapter 20

Carlita tossed and turned all night, visions of the armed robbers returning and breaking into the pawnshop filled her head. Maybe she'd been wrong to open a pawnshop. More than one person had told her it would attract a criminal element and they were right.

She remembered how Detective Polivich had told her Paradise Pawn had also been a target. Carlita wondered if they'd been robbed as well. She made a mental note to contact the detective the next morning to let him know what had happened.

It was possible he already knew since Detectives Polivich and Jackson worked at the same precinct...at least she thought they did.

The first slivers of daylight peeked in through a gap in Carlita's bedroom curtain. She gave up trying to go back to sleep, crawled out of bed and tiptoed into the living room.

Grayvie, who slept at the end of Carlita's bed, followed her out.

Rambo was sound asleep on the floor. He barely stirred as she passed by. "Some guard dog you are," she whispered as she made her way to the kitchen to start a pot of coffee.

Mercedes tromped into the kitchen a short time later and headed to the cupboard where she pulled out two clean coffee cups.

"You're up early."

"I am," Mercedes said. "There's been a change of plans." She poured coffee into both cups and handed one to her mother. "I set up the surveillance camera so we can watch it from either my computer or your laptop."

"Does Tony still have access to the surveillance?"

"Yep."

"That's a good idea. Three sets of eyes are better than one."

"So my plan is for you to stay up here and keep an eye on the cameras. I'll help Tony down in the store," Mercedes said.

"I have to sit up here all morning and stare at a computer screen?" Carlita asked.

"Not all day," Mercedes said. "Just for a little while."

After finishing their cups of coffee, mother and daughter took turns getting ready for what Carlita was certain would be a long day. They finished up just in time to head downstairs and met Tony in the hall. "You're right on time. I won't have to write you up for being late for work," he teased.

He turned to his sister. "Isn't this a little early for you?"

Mercedes punched her brother in the arm. "I get a lot less sleep than you. I just do my sleeping in the late morning."

Tony, who was carrying the cash register drawer, led them into the store. "From what I can tell, the crooks got away with about three grand in cash and whatever merchandise they took. We had a good day yesterday, too. I had to dig into our slush fund so we would have enough money to open for business today."

Mercedes walked past the empty, broken cabinet to the one she'd stored the merchandise inside. "There are a bunch of empty ring slots so it looks like they got away with some expensive jewelry too." She slipped her wristlet key ring off, unlocked the cabinet and began moving some of the ring displays to the damaged case.

Tony crossed the room and watched his sister. "What are you doing? The cabinet is broken."

"Exactly. That's why I'm moving merchandise into it."

"So someone can steal more merchandise?" he asked in disbelief.

"Sort of." Mercedes continued moving merchandise.

After she finished moving the merchandise, she tidied up the mess the robbers had made and then wandered to the back. "I'm going to work with you while Ma watches the surveillance cameras. I did a little finagling and now both she and I can keep an eye on the store using our computers."

Carlita turned the sign to *Open* and customers followed her into the store. The next couple of hours were busy as customers shopped and bought and with every purchase, Carlita felt a little better. They would recover from the robbery. She hoped Josh and Adele would, too.

When it got close to eleven, Mercedes asked her mother to run upstairs to keep an eye on the surveillance cameras.

Carlita headed upstairs and a few moments later, Adele entered the store.

A concerned Mercedes met the woman near the front. "How are you doing Adele? I was going to call earlier to make sure you didn't want to just stay home but we go so busy I forgot."

"I-I'm okay." Adele slipped her jacket off and carried it to the coatrack in the back. "I didn't sleep much last night, but mostly because I was worried about Josh. I called the hospital this morning. They're going to keep him until tomorrow so after I get off work I'm going to go visit him."

"Ma and I are going, too," Mercedes said. They chatted for a few moments and then Mercedes interrupted. "I'm glad to see you're okay." She told her brother and Adele she was heading upstairs and then wandered out of the store as more shoppers came in.

Her mother was sitting at the computer, watching the store on her laptop screen. "I see Adele made it in today. How is she doing?"

"She seems to be okay. She said she called the hospital. They're going to keep Josh for another day. He must've taken a pretty hard blow to the noggin."

Mercedes pulled her cell phone from her back pocket. "It's time for operation *Catch the Thief*."

She scrolled through the screen and dialed Tony's cell phone. "Tony. It's me, Mercedes. I need you to come up here right away. Mom needs your help!" She disconnected the line.

"I need help?" Carlita shook her head. "I'm confused."

"You'll see."

Seconds later, the door flew open and Tony raced into the living room. "What's wrong with Ma?" His eyes shifted from his sister to his mother.

Carlita shook her head. "I have no idea."

Mercedes motioned him to the desk. "If my calculations are correct, Adele will go right for the open jewelry display case and help herself."

"She's waiting on a customer," Carlita said. "Should we be leaving her all alone down there?"

"She'll be fine," Mercedes said.

It took forever for the customer to peruse the electronics section. He left without purchasing a single item. When he exited, he passed another customer who entered the store.

"Ugh. Go away." Mercedes told the shopper.

Finally, he left and Adele was alone on the store floor. As soon as the customer exited, the employee glanced around the store and walked to the back. Without warning, the camera went blank.

"The camera," Tony said. "She's playing games." He headed toward the door.

"Wait!" Mercedes yelled. "We need to give her a couple minutes."

Carlita stared at the blank screen in disbelief, her mind not registering what she'd just seen. "But how?"

"Let's call Detective Jackson and Detective Polivich," Mercedes said. She turned to her brother. "In the meantime, you go down and act as if nothing happened. Tell her Ma took a spill and we were worried she sprained her ankle or something."

"What I would like to do is wring her neck," Tony said.

"Stay cool, bro. She'll get hers. I'll be right there."

Tony exited the apartment while Carlita placed a call to both detectives. Detective Polivich didn't pick up but Detective Jackson did. She briefly told him they had a lead in the previous night's robbery and asked him to stop by Savannah Swag as soon as possible.

"I'm wrapping up another investigation," the detective said. "I'll be there within the hour."

"We'll be waiting." She disconnected the line and turned to her daughter. "What's this all about?"

"You'll see soon enough."

Mercedes and Carlita made their way to the store. To Tony's credit, he remained calm, acting as if nothing had happened and that his employee hadn't possibly tampered with the surveillance camera.

Mercedes wandered over to the coatrack where Adele had hung her jacket and casually ran her hand over the pockets. They were empty.

Next, she meandered over to the broken jewelry display where she studied the contents of the case. Earlier, before heading upstairs, Mercedes had taken a picture of the items inside. She reached into her pocket, switched her cell phone on and studied the picture she'd taken less than an hour ago.

She compared the photo to the contents and found there were two items missing - a stainless steel black diamond men's Rolex watch and a Cartier gold trinity diamond necklace.

Mercedes slipped the phone back inside her pocket and made a beeline for the cash register and receipts. She carefully checked the stack of the morning's receipts twice and couldn't find anything on the watch or the necklace.

She could feel eyes on her and she spun around to find Adele standing behind her. "Can I help you find something?"

"I hope so. I'm looking for the sales receipts for the black diamond men's Rolex watch and a Cartier gold trinity diamond necklace. Both were in the display case this morning and now they're gone," Mercedes said. "I don't see receipts for the sales."

Adele's eyes widened as she stared at the receipts Mercedes was holding. "Why...I have no idea. I didn't sell a Rolex or Cartier necklace.

Maybe you sold them and misplaced the receipts."

Mercedes set the receipts on the counter, reached into her back pocket and pulled out her cell phone. She pulled up the picture of the display case she'd taken earlier. "No. They were here this morning, right before I went upstairs."

Tony and Carlita, overhearing the conversation, made their way over.

Mercedes turned to her brother. "You and Ma were the only other two working this morning. Did either of you sell an expensive Rolex watch or Cartier diamond necklace?"

Tony shook his head. "No way. I would remember that."

Mercedes shifted her gaze and lowered her voice. "What did you do with them Adele?"

"I-I don't know what you're talking about." She took a step back. "I shouldn't have come to work. I'm feeling ill now."

"Are they in your pocket?" Mercedes glanced at Adele's front pockets. They looked empty. "Please turn around so I can see your back pockets."

"No!" Adele shifted to the side and reached for her jacket, hanging on the hook. "You think I stole those items. I quit and I'm going to sue you for emotional distress from last night's robbery!"

Adele snatched her jacket off the hook and started for the door.

"Stop her!" Mercedes said, but it wasn't necessary. The timing was perfect and Detective Jackson was making his way inside.

Chapter 21

Adele attempted to slip past the detective.

Mercedes hurried after her. "Stop her!"

Detective Jackson stuck his arm out. "I think she means you. Let's go back inside." He led her to the back.

Adele's face puckered, as if she were going to start bawling. Mercedes quickly dismissed the tears. "Save the waterworks for the judge." She turned to Detective Jackson. "It appears our employee here, Ms. Adele Ketman, is somehow involved in the string of burglaries."

She pointed at Adele. "Empty your pockets."

"No. I will not." Adele's expression grew defiant.

"What's in her pockets?" the detective asked.

"Merchandise our employee stole from us this morning while we weren't around," Mercedes said.

"She's lying," Adele said. "I think she's stealing from her own business and trying to blame it on innocent employees."

The detective lifted a brow. "Then you will have no problem emptying all of your pockets."

Adele's eyes widened. "I..."

"Do it here or do it down at the police station," Detective Jackson said.

Adele's eyes rolled back in her head and in a great display of hysterics promptly fell into a heap on the floor.

"This makes it easier." Mercedes reached for her pocket.

"No." The detective shook his head as he studied Adele. "We need something to bring her around. I'll be right back."

Carlita watched as he made his way to the passenger side of his unmarked police car, open the door and reach inside. He returned moments later, carrying a small cylinder.

The detective removed the lid and waved it in front of Adele's nose. She began to gag and cough before opening her eyes.

"Ah. Glad to see you're all right." He helped her to her feet. "Now where were we?" He snapped his fingers. "You were just about to empty your pockets."

Adele scowled at Mercedes before reaching into her back pockets. "I told you. I did not steal anything and now I'm going to sue all of you." She pointed at the detective. "You too."

"I...don't understand." Mercedes shook her head. "The merchandise is gone. She messed up the camera so we wouldn't see what she was doing." Her eyes narrowed. "There is one more place we haven't checked."

"Her bra," Carlita and Mercedes said in unison.

The look on Adele's face told them they were on the right track. "If you touch me, I'll sue."

Detective Jackson shifted his feet. "Have it your way. Down to the precinct we go. We'll get to the bottom of this one way or another."

Adele stepped back. "On what grounds?"

"We'll start with resisting arrest," Detective Jackson said as he attempted to handcuff a squirming Adele.

Mercedes thought Adele would give up the gig but she protested the entire time the detective read her her rights and cuffed her before leading her to the unmarked police car. After she was safely inside and the doors shut, he returned. "I'll give her a few minutes to cool off. Do you have any other evidence?"

Mercedes showed the detective the surveillance tape and the part where Adele walked over to the wall and the screen went blank. "I started to suspect it was her after last night's armed robbery. She wasn't injured but our other employee was knocked out."

"Motive and opportunity. She and her partners were selling merchandise not only to us, but also the other local pawnshops," Mercedes said. "They would rob homes and then have their partners bring the merchandise in to sell. A couple days later, another accomplice would come into the business, claiming they'd been robbed, identifying the items and then getting the merchandise back."

The detective rubbed his chin thoughtfully. "They could then turn around and take the merchandise to another local pawnshop and repeat the crime."

"Tony called the bluff on the one and contacted the police. Detective Polivich started to get a little too close for comfort and Lyla

Crenshaw, one of the crooks, disappeared off the face of the earth."

Carlita began to pace back and forth. "So they decided to up the ante and planned an armed robbery. Adele would play victim, all the while being in on it."

She stopped abruptly. "What about Ben Cutler? He may be part of it as well."

"Nope." Mercedes shook her head. "I finally found out what SGCPO means. South Georgia Consumer Protection Office."

"They're a government agency that investigates crime rings," Detective Jackson said. "I don't know a Ben Cutler but I do know an Evan Cutler. Tall guy, thin with dark hair."

"So he was secretly investigating us while we were investigating him," Mercedes said.

"How were you investigating him?"

"Uh, well not really investigating," Mercedes backtracked. "I...we."

"On his application, Cutler listed his employer as the IRS and then told me he worked at the office downtown. When we found out they had no idea who he was or who his supervisor was, we began to grow suspicious and decided to do a little digging. He kept popping up everywhere," Carlita explained.

Detective Jackson glanced out the front window at his car. Adele was in the back seat, banging her head against the glass window. "I better get her down to the station before she hurts herself."

The detective strode out of the store and to his car where he opened the driver's side door and leaned in as he talked to Adele. Moments later, he climbed behind the wheel and they sped off.

Mercedes shook her head. "Hopefully she'll decide to save her own neck and start talking. All this time she's been tampering with merchandise, making Tony question his inventory counts. She was stealing merchandise and when I did the inventory, it was off. We may have never found out the truth if I hadn't set the bait by leaving the jewelry ripe for the picking. She knew I hadn't had time to inventory what was stolen last night so she helped herself."

"She also knew we have the video surveillance so she kept pulling the wire when she was ready to commit a crime." Mercedes continued. "Then she tried to pin it on Ben Cutler."

"I'm partly to blame for that," Carlita said. "I pointed him out to her and told her to keep an eye on him."

"Which made him the perfect scapegoat," Mercedes said.

"Maybe you should write a crime novel," Carlita teased.

"I might just do that," Mercedes shot back as she grinned at her mother.

Chapter 22

"I signed a crooked contract y'all,

Yesterday I was worried, looking for a new place to live,

Until an angel named Elvira, found me a place to eat and sleep,

Her skin is flawless, her figure fine,

If she was my girlfriend, I would be on Cloud 9."

Carlita chuckled at the words to Cool Bones' song. She could've sworn that Elvira, who was standing not far from the stage, started to swoon.

After the song ended, the throng of guests clapped loudly and Cool Bones and the Jazz Boys began a second song, this one slower. They lowered the stage lights and Carlita gazed up at the twinkling string lights that dotted the courtyard trees.

Couples began to make their way onto the small dance floor Carlita had carved out for guests.

"May I have this dance?" a deep voice whispered in her ear.

Carlita's heart skipped a beat. John Alder stood behind her, a smile on his face as he extended his hand.

"O-of course." Carlita placed her hand in his. He gently squeezed it as he placed his arm across her back and led her to the floor.

Glenda Bell, who was dancing with her husband, winked when she caught a glimpse of the couple.

Carlita's cheeks warmed and she was glad it was dark as John pulled her closer and they began to circle the floor. She closed her eyes briefly and caught a whiff of his cologne, a combination of leather and musk. It had been a long time since Carlita had been this close to a man, other than her sons.

John leaned in. "You look lovely tonight, Carlita. Your dress matches the sparkle in your fiery Italian eyes."

Carlita smiled at John's attempt to lighten the moment. "Thank you...I think."

All too soon, the song ended and John released his grip on Carlita. "Thank you for indulging me."

"Thank you for asking me," she whispered.

"There you are!" Mercedes interrupted their moment. "We have to run upstairs and grab more appetizers. We're already out."

Mercedes and Carlita reloaded their trays of goodies and carried them around the courtyard, offering the tasty treats to guests while Tony and Autumn offered glasses of wine and champagne.

The first part of the dinner party flew by, thanks in part to Cool Bones and the Jazz Boys.

Several of the guests picked up the band's business cards and Carlita could tell Cool Bones was thrilled with the enthusiasm of the crowd.

The courtyard was packed and all too soon, Cool Bones and his band had to leave. It was time for them to head down to the *Thirsty Crow* for their real job but not before Carlita stopped them near the courtyard gate.

She gave each of them a gift card to one of the riverfront restaurants and promised she would stop by soon to listen to them play.

The party transitioned smoothly to the upper hall where Annie and Cindi had offered to lend a hand setting out the dishes for the dinner part of the party.

The guests mingled and chatted while Violet, Shelby's young daughter, handed out yellow roses to each of the female guests.

Carlita had decided it would be a nice touch and Violet was thrilled with her important task. She was even more excited when Carlita told her to keep two...one for her mother and one for her.

The evening flew by and before she knew it, the guests began to leave, each one thanking her for a wonderful evening.

By the time the last guest departed, Carlita's feet were sore and her face hurt from smiling. It had been a wonderful evening and nearly perfect in every way.

Shelby offered to help clean up but Violet was rubbing her eyes. "You go on dear. I know you have to work in the morning. I appreciate your patience in letting me host the party in the hall."

"It was a great party." Shelby hugged Carlita.

Violet hopped into Carlita's arms and hugged her neck. "It was the bestest." She placed the palms of her small hands on Carlita's cheeks and her expression grew solemn. "Can I call you Nana?"

Carlita's eyes watered and her throat clogged as she looked into two precious blue eyes. "Of course you can," she whispered and then gently hugged the small child. "Nana it is."

Violet grabbed her mother's hand and then skipped inside their apartment. Shelby's lower lip quivered and she smiled at Carlita before slowly closing their apartment door.

"I think you need more grandkids." Mercedes snuck up next to her mother. "A few who live closer to you than Paulie's tribe."

Carlita tilted her head and studied her daughter. "You better find a boyfriend first."

"Not me." Mercedes rolled her eyes. "Tony. Just think of the adorable children he and Shelby would have."

"Yes, they would be adorable, wouldn't they?" Carlita placed her hands on her hips and surveyed what was left of the party...dirty appetizer plates, overflowing trashcans and scraps of leftovers. "It got so hectic earlier; I forgot to tell you that Detective Jackson called."

"What did he say?"

"That a defiant Adele finally coughed up the jewelry inside her bra," Carlita said.

"I knew it!" Mercedes interrupted.

"In exchange for a plea deal and naming her accomplices, she also confessed to being part of a theft ring, which included Lyla Crenshaw and the fictitious Dawson Greene, among others. They're still in the process of investigating but have already searched Adele and her *boyfriend* Sam's apartment."

"So there was no ill grandfather?" Mercedes asked.

"Nope." Carlita shook her head. "You'll never guess where the boyfriend, Sam, works."

She didn't give her daughter time to answer. "Paradise Pawn."

"That figures."

Carlita began stacking the plates. "They recovered some cash and merchandise and are hoping once they are able to search the other accomplices' premises, they'll recover more." She set the plates off to the side and tugged on the end of the tablecloth. "Unfortunately that won't help us since the merchandise will be returned to the rightful owners."

"But we may get some of the cash," Mercedes pointed out.

"True. But I'm not holding my breath."

Tony, who had been downstairs checking on the pawnshop, tromped up the steps, having caught the tail end of the conversation. "Good riddance," he muttered. "Adele better never show her face around here again." He began bagging up the trash.

"Let's start putting away the dessert table first," Mercedes told her mother.

"What's left of it." Carlita gazed at the empty cookie platter and cheesecake tray. There was one small slice of hummingbird cake left.

"Did you try the cake?" Mercedes asked.

"Only a spoonful of frosting when I was cleaning the bowl. Eating a piece is supposed to bring you good luck."

Mercedes grabbed three forks and handed one to her mother and one to her brother, who had returned from trash duty. "We need all the help we can get."

Carlita carved off a piece and popped it into her mouth. The cream cheese frosting and walnuts were mixed with just the right amount of pineapple and banana. "This is so good."

"We'll have to make it again." Mercedes waited for her mother to take another fork full before polishing it off. "On a more serious note, this was a fabulous blowout Ma," she said as she grabbed the end of the folding table and tipped it on its side. "I can't wait to see what happens when you open your restaurant."

"Me either," Tony chimed in.

Carlita groaned. "One day at a time, you two. One day at a time."

The end.

The Series Continues...Look for Book 6 in the "Made in Savannah" Series Coming Soon!

Get Free Books and More!

Sign up for my Free Cozy Mysteries Newsletter to get free and discounted books, giveaways & soon-to-be-released books!

hopecallaghan.com/newsletter

Meet The Author

Hope Callaghan is an author who loves to write Christian books, especially Christian Mystery and Cozy Mystery books. <u>She has written more than 50 mystery books (and counting)</u> in five series.

Born and raised in a small town in West Michigan, she now lives in Florida with her husband.

She is the proud mother of one daughter and a stepdaughter and stepson. When she's not doing the thing she loves best - writing books - she enjoys cooking, traveling and reading books.

Hope loves to connect with her readers! Connect with her today!

Visit **hopecallaghan.com** for special offers, free books, and soon-to-be-released books!

Email: <u>hope@hopecallaghan.com</u>

Facebook:
<u>https://www.facebook.com/hopecallaghanauthor/</u>

Hummingbird Cake Recipe

3 cups all-purpose flour

2 cups white granulated sugar

1 teaspoon baking soda

1 teaspoon salt

3/4 teaspoon cinnamon

1-1/2 cups canola oil

3 eggs

1 – 8 oz. can crushed pineapple, drained (reserve ½ tsp for frosting - optional)

2 cups mashed bananas

1 cup chopped walnuts

1 tsp. vanilla extract

2 – 8 oz. packages cream cheese, softened

¼ lb. butter (one stick), softened

2-1/2 cups powdered sugar

Directions:

Preheat oven to 350 degrees. Grease and flour

two 9-inch cake pans.

In large bowl, mix flour, granulated sugar, baking soda, salt and ½ tsp cinnamon.

In smaller bowl, combine oil, eggs, pineapple, bananas, ½ tsp vanilla and ½ cup chopped nuts (keep other ½ cup to sprinkle on frosting).

Pour batter evenly into the greased/floured cake pans.

Bake in preheated oven for 45 minutes (or 1 hour) or until toothpick inserted in center comes out clean. Remove cakes from oven, set aside to cool.

Prepare frosting: Blend cream cheese, butter, powdered sugar, ½ tsp. vanilla and ¼ tsp. cinnamon until smooth. Add pineapple juice (optional.)

Remove cooled cakes from cake pans. Center one cake on round plate. Spread icing on top and sprinkle a few nuts on top. Place second cake on top of first frosted cake. Frost top and sides, and then sprinkle with remaining walnuts.

Carlita's Linguine Recipe

<u>Ingredients</u>:

2 tablespoons olive oil

6 cloves garlic, crushed

4 cups whole peeled tomatoes, with liquid, chopped

12 Castelvetrano olives, chopped

1-1/2 tsp. salt

1 tsp. Italian seasoning

8 oz. of linguine pasta

Grated or shredded parmesan

Fresh basil

<u>Directions</u>:

In a large saucepan, heat 2 tablespoons olive oil with garlic over medium heat.

When garlic starts to sizzle, pour chopped tomatoes and chopped green olives into mixture.

Add salt and Italian seasoning. Stir.
Simmer for 15 minutes, stirring occasionally.

While tomatoes simmer, bring large pot of water to boil. Cook pasta 8-10 minutes or until al dente.
Add cooked pasta to saucepan. Cook 3 – 4 minutes or until sauce begins to boil.

After plated, sprinkle grated/shredded parmesan on top. Garnish with fresh basil.

CPSIA information can be obtained
at www.ICGtesting.com
Printed in the USA
LVHW032231170423
744627LV00016B/111